*"But you can't leave now..*

I'm just about to strike oil!"

"That's what you've told me twice before." Cleo spun around to face Tom squarely. "Why don't you stop this foolishness? There's no oil on this ranch! There's nothing but rattlesnakes and sand! And the few cattle we have left are only here by dumb luck."

She paused and began to pace. "Stop and think, Tom. Even if you do hit oil, do you except me to raise our daughter in this solitude? No children to play with. No decent school. Nothing but loneliness. Let's go back to Houston," she begged. "You can get a good job with J. J. there, and we'd be able to give Claire all the things she's entitled to. Do you remember how lonely it was for you growing up out here? And you had Robert."

Her eyes pled with him as she turned to regard him and then the bitterness spewed forth. "I despise this place, Tom! If I stay here any longer, I'll soon look just like your mother. Have you taken a good look at her lately? She's like one of those mesquites in wintertime. Is that what you want for me? For your daughter?

"Tom, you're responsible for two people in this world— Claire and me. How do you plan to take care of us?"

**LINDA HERRING** is the mother of four grown children and the wife of a Lutheran minister. Her writing is an avenue of ministry whereby she both entertains and uplifts with her down-to-earth view of Christianity.

**Books by Linda Herring**

HEARTSONG PRESENTS

HP49—Yesterday's Tomorrows

# Song of Captivity

## Linda Herring

*Heartsong Presents*

*To Perry,*
*who led me through my captivity.*

ISBN 1-55748-510-0

SONG OF CAPTIVITY

## *one*

### Summer, 1925
### Galveston Beach

She was twenty that summer. Curled up under the beach umbrella, she watched him from beneath the small hat pulled down over her ebony hair. The harsh glare of the sun caused her to squint, and she raised her hand to shade her eyes.

He was laughing, trying to duck his male companion under the gentle swell of the waves. His muscles gleamed as the water streamed off his lithe body. Then as his friend lost his footing, he threw back his head in a jubilant guffaw, and a strand of dark hair fell into his eyes. He lifted a careless hand to brush it away from his face. Pausing a moment, he glanced toward the shore, as if he felt her watching him. At that moment his friend came up, gasping for air, shouting threats and lunging for him in retaliation.

"Ooo, he's divine," breathed her friend Mattie.

Cleo smiled a slow, secretive smile, and nodded.

"Do you know him?" Mattie shifted on the blanket, careful to stay out of the sun's rays.

"Not yet," Cleo replied in her low voice.

"You aren't going to try to arrange a meeting, are you?" Distaste colored Mattie's tone. "That's so common." She checked her pale skin for signs of reddening.

"You know me better than that!" There was an air of injured dignity in Cleo's tone. "I've never picked up a man in my life."

"I know that you play with fire and skirt the rules whenever you can," snorted Mattie.

"Don't be such a bluenose." Cleo didn't contest her friend's statement. Her innocent antics were what made her life bearable, helped her endure her parents' tiresome moral and social code. But their status in the community was firm, and they wouldn't tolerate serious misbehavior on the part of their only daughter.

For Cleo, however, Christianity was a set of outdated rules, a moralistic code that seemed Victorian to her. She prayed erratically, and then usually only to plead to be excused from the wages of her sins.

As Cleo watched the man at play in the water with his friend, something deep inside contracted with excitement. A distant ache. A silent fluttering. He was most handsome, and the dark woolen bathing costume enhanced his well-proportioned physique.

Mattie eyed the sun, inching toward the westward horizon in sedate summer fashion. "We need to think about going back to Houston. It will be dinnertime soon." She arched her thinly penciled eyebrows. "Are you listening to me, Cleo Seachrist?"

"Hmmm." Cleo didn't take her eyes off the figure of the man. "What do you suppose it's like to really be in love?"

Mattie's gaze followed Cleo's out to the swelling waves. "That sort of man always looks dangerous to me. I want to wear white to my wedding and have it mean something." She looked again at her friend, reclining gracefully on the sand. "Don't you?"

Cleo was thoughtful. "I suppose. But what I really want is to be madly in love." Her deep blue eyes glittered with intensity. "Think how exciting it would be. How romantic. To love someone enough to . . . to give yourself to him."

Mattie's mouth circled in a surprised "O."

"Don't you want to love someone like that?" Cleo asked.

"Yes, of course, but my conscience wouldn't let me,"

Mattie assured her. "It would be wrong."

Cleo smiled ruefully at the warning note she had heard so often from her mother. "Let's go home. I've heard that sermon before."

Mattie got up huffily, dusting off the sand from her bathing costume. "Honestly, Cleo, sometimes you make me so mad." She looked down at her best friend, who was gathering up the umbrella. "And frankly, sometimes you worry me," she added, wrinkling her brow.

Cleo's laugh was husky. "Oh, don't worry. I'm not going to run away with a stranger. I've got a family, too." She threw one last longing look over her shoulder and sighed.

The two young women didn't go back to Galveston Beach that week, for the early spring weather turned cool and rainy. But Cleo had an idea. One that made Mattie's mouth circle in the astonished "O" once more. It took some persuading, but Cleo had always been good at that, and soon even Mattie was caught up in the spirit of adventure. Still, Mother would probably need her smelling salts when she found out about this escapade!

Cleo felt a rush of excitement as she and Mattie stood in line at the public bathhouse on Galveston Beach, waiting to rent a swimming costume. When her turn at the window came, she spoke clearly and distinctly, "A man's swimsuit, please." With a delicious flutter of anticipation, she noted the look of shocked disapproval on the clerk's face and heard a slight gasp of surprise from someone in the line behind her. She paid her money and accepted the suit, then stood aside for Mattie to step up to the window. Cleo gave Mattie a conspiratorial look as her friend made the identical request.

Ignoring the stares that followed their departure, they entered one of the small dressing rooms.

"You aren't going to back out on me, are you?" Cleo asked as she shucked off her dress.

"I don't think so, but my heart is beating ninety miles an hour. Did you see those shocked faces? Cleo, are you sure . . .?"

A throaty laugh accompanied Cleo's delighted smile. "Just wait 'til we parade around in the Bathing Beauty Review!" She smoothed down the fabric of the swimsuit and struck an exaggerated pose, hands on her boyish hips, one knee cocked upward slightly, head tipped to the side. "How do I look?"

"Smashing, of course." A frown creased Mattie's smooth brow. "Do you think we'll get arrested?"

Cleo laughed her husky laugh once more. "Are you crazy? Only our arms are exposed. Besides, this is 1925, not the gay '90s. And it's Galveston Splash Day, the first day of the summer season. Everyone will be wearing these cute suits. Come on, Mattie, they don't enforce that old law about being covered from elbow to knees any more. This is the twentieth century."

"Yeah, you'd better hope the police know what year it is," Mattie said darkly. She smoothed the close-fitting cloche over her fiery red hair, while Cleo put on the ankle-high shoes that were designed for the bathing costumes.

That familiar tingle of daring rippled through Cleo again, and she winked at Mattie.

"What now?"

"I was thinking how embarrassed my dear sainted mother would be if she could see her only child now." Unconsciously her hand went to the scooped neckline of the garment, tugging it upwards a little.

Mattie pulled the mid-thigh legs of her brightly striped suit. "I'll probably get sunburned. Redheads never tan."

Cleo wrapped an emerald green headband around her

coal-black bob and inspected her own milky complexion in the dressing room mirror. "Oh, fiddlesticks! We can rent an umbrella." She sighed. "Well, this is it."

Firmly she pushed open the door, which made an alarmingly loud thud as it crashed into a very attractive young man standing just outside. "Oh, I'm so sorry!" she apologized quickly.

"No problem, ma'am," he drawled, his eyes large pools of chocolate brown. "Such a pretty young lady can run me down anytime." Even his grin was lazy, curling full lips above very white teeth.

She recognized him as the man she had seen playing in the waves several weeks earlier. "How very gallant," she murmured, acknowledging his grin with a coy look.

He nodded and passed by. If he had been wearing a hat, he would have tipped it, Cleo thought, easily imagining him in a gray Stetson.

"He's gorgeous!" exploded Mattie as they watched his muscular frame disappear in the direction of the beach. "He's the one, isn't he? The one we saw last time?"

Cleo nodded. "And he's even more handsome up close. Come on." She started in the same direction he had just taken.

"Cleo, for pity sakes! You can't follow him!"

"Don't be silly. We have to go this way to enter the contest." But there was a predatory gleam in the dark blue eyes that did not escape Mattie's notice. "How very fortunate," she murmured.

Cleo had been partially right. There were a few women dressed as they were, but the vast majority of them still wore the modest addition of skirt and stockings.

"Ohhh," Mattie groaned, "why ever did I let you talk me into this?"

"Isn't this fun?" purred Cleo softly as they lined up to get their sashes for the contest. Scanning the bevy of hopefuls, she decided that there was only one other girl who might be real competition.

So Cleo wasn't surprised when she won first place. She had been exclaimed over from the cradle, pampered and catered to from infancy. She accepted the little crown and the photographer's plea for one more shot for the *Galveston Daily News.*

"Your mother's going to kill us when she sees this in the paper," Mattie fretted. "I should have known this would get us into trouble. My mother will know right away that I was with you. Ohhh, Cleo, did you have to win first place?"

"I doubt very seriously that the Houston paper will run a story on Galveston's Splash Day," said Cleo. "There's too much competition between the two cities. Houston isn't going to advertise for Galveston. Come on, Mattie, where's your sense of adventure?"

"Probably on the front page," she answered gloomily.

"Come on, old girl, let's go get something cool to drink."

"Only if you take off that crown. You look like a deposed monarch advertising for a job."

Cleo laughed and accommodated her friend.

There were plenty of opportunities for discreet flirtations. The recent notoriety of their participation in the beauty contest had people pointing them out and young men making attempts to catch their attention. They kept the men at arm's length with practiced ease.

For the rest of the afternoon, the two young women played at the edge of the water, dodging the greedy waves licking at their shoes, and then settled in the shade at the base of the seventeen-foot-high seawall with their iced drinks.

"You're getting a bit pink," observed Cleo.

"So are you. Hmmm, this shade feels nice. We should have found it an hour ago. I'll probably peel like a molting lobster."

"Don't look now, but that good-looking cowboy is heading this way." Cleo shifted a little on the sand, adjusting her bathing costume modestly.

He stopped at their umbrella and peered under. "Congratulations," he said to Cleo.

"Thank you. Aren't you the young man I crashed into at the bathhouse?"

"I'm honored, ma'am, that the reigning beauty queen remembers me." He offered his hand. "I'm Tom Kinney."

She took his strong hand in her own, "Cleo Seachrist and this is my friend, Mattie Meyers."

Mattie and Tom exchanged nods and Tom added, "Pleased to meet you, too, ma'am. I'm sure the judges had a hard time making up their minds."

Mattie laughed out loud. "This one's a keeper, Cleo!"

Tom turned his attention back to Cleo. "Are you from Galveston, Miss Seachrist?"

She could smell the salt water coming from his wet suit. His hair was damp and hung in careless waves, combed by the ocean breezes. "Ah, no. We're both from Houston and go to the university in Austin."

His eyes held hers, closing out the rest of the world. "I never got to go to college," he confessed. "I joined up for the war instead, and when I got out, I got a job as a ship's mechanic here on the wharves." He was not unaware of her assessing gaze traveling over his well-muscled frame, however covert it might be.

"Was it exciting, Mr. Kinney . . . the war, I mean?" she asked.

"Sometimes. Mostly it was scary or boring. So I wasn't too concerned when I got gassed with mustard gas . . . just enough to be sent home."

Mattie intruded into their private conversation. "It must

have been wonderful seeing all those foreign countries."

He turned slightly, giving Cleo a view of his profile. "Not *that* way."

"I guess it would be a little different from going as a tourist," Mattie admitted.

"I'd like to go back to visit England someday."

"Cleo and I will be going to England in August."

"Is that so, Miss Seachrist?" The man's lazy Texas drawl was in perfect cadence with the casual glance he sent her way.

Cleo felt herself responding to his attention. "Yes. My father has business there. Perhaps we'll see you." Her frank look told him she'd like that.

He shrugged. "I doubt it. It'll take me a long time to save enough for a trip like that. Maybe someday. I do get to Houston to see my aunt once in a while, though," he added. "Would you mind if I called on you? We could have dinner."

"By all means." Her smile was genuine.

"'Til then, ladies." Tom rose and waved as he walked toward the bathhouses.

"Your mother will go into cardiac arrest," Mattie said flatly as soon as he was out of earshot. "There's no way she's going to let you go out with a ship's mechanic."

"Mattie, you know I'm world class in getting my way with my parents. You just have to know which buttons to push." Cleo watched Tom's disappearing form. "Isn't he something? All those beautiful muscles. And that face. Even Mother will be impressed."

Mattie's face registered total disbelief at that statement. "Your mother knows rhinestones from diamonds, sweetie. You'd better hope he doesn't come calling in jeans and a cowboy hat."

"Hmmm," said Cleo, imagining the effect.

Mattie frowned. "Are you getting in over your head again, Cleo? I thought you'd learned your lesson with that down-and-out artist you dragged home to meet your folks."

Cleo stuck out her tongue. "This one will be worth the effort," she assured her friend. "Mark my words."

Mattie touched her fair skin with a tentative finger. "I need to get out of this sun. I'm burning for sure. Even an umbrella can't help me now. Come on, Juliet, let's get dressed."

The two women ignored the looks of disapproval cast by the modestly dressed women on the beach and made their way back to the bathhouses.

As they changed, Cleo practiced the story she would tell her mother and father about entering the contest.

"Honestly, Cleo, you spend more time covering your tracks than a renegade Indian," Mattie complained. "Why do you do these things?"

"Because I hate sameness, you old stick in the mud! Where is your daring? Are you going to be bored out of your mind until they put you in the ground?"

"Not with you around. But I'll probably wind up in prison . . . or worse, disinherited by my folks!" Mattie laughed in spite of herself. With Cleo, she never lacked for excitement. "You're not a bad girl, but you do seem to have a knack for living on the edge."

Cleo gave her friend a loving look. "You know me pretty well, don't you? Why do you put up with me?"

"Because I was appointed by God to be your guardian angel. That's the only reason I stay around . . . because I know He'll call me to account if I don't!" She heaved an overdone sigh. "I only hope I pass the test."

"Me, too," Cleo agreed.

They returned their damp suits and found Cleo's smart little Model A Ford parked on top of the seawall. Soon they were crossing the narrow causeway over Galveston Bay and watching the boats bob around in the smooth green water as they made their way back to Houston. It was already dusk, and Cleo pushed the car as fast as it would go. The salty air on her forehead was soothing.

"I do intend to see him again, you know," she told Mattie.

"I know." Mattie's eyes mirrored her concern. "Just don't do anything stupid. Please?"

Cleo smiled. She was replaying the moment of their first meeting, seeing the young man's strong features. Once again that familiar feeling stirred. Something unfulfilled, untasted. Each time she met an attractive man, it was the same. Was this the one who would satisfy her girlhood longings? Was this the man she would marry?

"I recognize that smile," Mattie said.

"Do you?"

"Of course. It's your "someday-my-prince-will-come" smile. Cleo," Mattie said, turning a solemn look in her friend's direction, "God will send you the right man . . . in His good time. Maybe even soon. And it will be someone you can take home without a problem." Her eyes lit up. "What's wrong with Bob? He's crazy about you."

Cleo dismissed the suggestion with a wave of her hand. "Bob is a bore . . . so immature." Then she spoke more hesitantly. "Mattie . . . do you really believe that God still does things for people? I mean, don't you think He more or less just sets things in motion and sits back and watches us run around trying to find the answers?"

Mattie sighed, this time with genuine concern. "I think He still takes care of us, and you wouldn't feel so insecure if you believed it, too. Why don't you just wait till God sends the right person? Maybe you'll even meet him in England. Wouldn't that be something?" she asked dreamily. "He might even have a title . . . Lord Somebody, not a nobody like that ship's mechanic."

Cleo shrugged. "You may be right, but I don't think even you could miss the totally masculine aura about Tom Kinney." She shivered in the hot, humid air as she braked to a stop in front of the well-tended grounds of Mattie's mansion.

"All I want is for you to be happy," Mattie said as she pulled her duffel bag from the back seat, her pink face screwed up with concern. "But I'm afraid this Tom Kinney is not going to give you what you're looking for."

"You worry too much," Cleo said with a laugh. "All I'm going to do is have dinner with him, *if* he calls."

"Oh, he'll call. He can spot a winner when he sees one." Mattie grinned reluctantly. "Speaking of winners, do you know what you're going to tell your family about the contest?"

"I do. And it's completely plausible. You?"

"'I'll tell my folks you drugged me and I didn't know what I was doing!"

"And I'll tell mine," Cleo mused, "that you talked me into it and I went along to protect you from nefarious fortune-hunters."

"*I* talked *you* into it?! You rat!" Mattie rolled her eyes. "No wonder your mother frowns when I come for tea. What must she think of me?"

"Oh, she'll only be mad for a day or two, then she'll be proud that I won a beauty contest. She loves me, you know."

"Yes, I know." Mattie nodded solemnly.

"Now I gotta get out of here. See you tomorrow."

"What are we going to do? Rob a bank?"

"I was thinking of going back to the beach. . . ." Cleo began, staring off into the distance.

"You aren't serious! I couldn't! I'd be burned to a crisp!"

"No, I'm not serious. I was really thinking we could go

shopping and spend some of my father's hard-earned money. I'll need some clothes for the trip."

When Mattie thought of all the clothes crammed into Cleo's closets, she laughed. But it would be fun to shop together. At least, she wouldn't have to worry about her friend running into that man in the department store.

At dinner that night in the family dining room, Cleo told her version of the contest, careful to give it a humorous slant to placate her mother's fears.

As the servants cleared the table, Mrs. Seachrist spoke up. "I trust you will not find it necessary to repeat this . . . escapade to any of our friends."

"Now, Mother," her distinguished husband spoke up, "it was only a girlish lark. No one need know."

"Unless it comes out in the paper," Cleo added impishly.

A well-manicured hand clutching an Irish linen napkin fluttered to Mrs. Seachrist's bosom. "The paper! Oh, surely not! You don't really think it will be in the paper!"

"Probably only in the Galveston paper, Mother," Cleo soothed. "With the picture."

Her mother closed her eyes as if in a swoon. "Oh, dear Lord in heaven," she prayed.

"Calm yourself, Mother," Mr. Seachrist put in, "the Houston paper isn't going to print some silly article. Not when there's real news to report."

*Typical,* thought Cleo. Her father would not consider anything that happened in the provincial hamlet of Galveston worthy of mention in a Houston newspaper. For all their sakes, she sincerely hoped he was right!

Cleo quickly cast about for a more appealing topic of conversation. "Mattie and I are going shopping tomorrow. Would you like to come along, Mother?"

Her mother seemed genuinely regretful when she had to decline. "I'd love to, dear, but I have another commitment.

The Garden Club is giving its spring tea. But you and Mattie run along. I'm sure you'll find some lovely things to wear in England when we see your father's business friends. One never knows whom one might meet." She arched one eyebrow in a meaningful wing.

It occurred to Cleo that for her mother, this little trip might be an all-out husband-hunting expedition, but she couldn't honestly say she was displeased with the notion. How romantic to marry an English gentleman and live in his castle. "May I be excused now, Mother? I'm a little tired."

"Of course, darling. And, Cleo," Mrs. Seachrist added, "do find something to put on your skin. You're going to look like a field hand if you get one of those awful suntans. You must take good care of your complexion, you know."

"Yes, Mother, I'll take care of it. I want it to look as marvelous as yours when I'm your age."

Mollified, Mrs. Seachrist accepted the soft kiss Cleo dropped on her forehead.

In her room, Cleo scattered her clothes in her dressing room for the maid to put away and walked into her bathroom. As she bathed, she decided that getting her parents to see Tom Kinney would be a little more difficult than she had led Mattie to believe it would be, especially if her mother discovered they had met on the beach without a proper introduction or chaperone. Maybe a double date with Mattie and J.J., she mused. That would be much easier to arrange.

She crawled into bed with a half-formed plan simmering in her mind and a short prayer that God would approve. *It can't hurt,* she thought. *Besides, Mattie might be right. Maybe God does answer prayers.* In any case, she wanted to cover all her bases.

# two

When Tom called a week later, Cleo was pleased, but not surprised. On the phone his conversation sounded real and down-to-earth rather than the contrived small talk she was accustomed to hearing from the boys she usually dated.

"Dinner? I'd love it," she agreed heartily the instant he mentioned seeing her again.

"What's your favorite restaurant?"

It crossed her mind that her favorite, Chez André, was quite expensive, surely beyond his means. "Why don't you suggest a place," she stalled.

"Is there any reason you might not want to be seen with me?" he said with a trace of unexplained anger in his voice.

"Don't be silly! I'd love to eat at Chez André with you." The fact that she knew the headwaiter might come in handy, too, she thought.

"Then I'll be by for you around eight." The timbre in his voice promised an exciting evening.

"I'm looking forward to it," she purred, hoping he hadn't guessed just how much.

She called Mattie as soon as she had hung up.

"Thus begins the drama," sighed her best friend. "What are you going to tell your folks about what he does for a living? I think all the shipping magnates are accounted for."

"Very funny, Mattie," Cleo observed wryly. "I'll introduce him and whisk him away before Mother has time to check out his portfolio."

"Good luck. The Lord knows you're going to need it. Where are you going?"

"Chez André."

Mattie laughed. "I can scarcely imagine a ship's mechanic in that place. So you're going to put him to the test right away, huh?" Her voice grew serious. "I do hope you know what you're doing, Cleo. He'll probably make a complete idiot out of himself, and if he does, he won't like you for that."

"I'm not testing him, Mattie," Cleo protested. "Not exactly, that is. Let's just say I'm giving him an opportunity to put his best foot forward."

"Well, it will certainly be an interesting evening. I hope *that* story doesn't wind up on the front page of the Houston paper."

"There's just one more tiny detail I neglected to mention," Cleo began hesitantly. "I need you and J.J. to go with us. You know I'll have a better chance with Mother if there's another couple along."

"Here we go again." Mattie couldn't resist toying with her friend. "The food is pretty good, but I don't know if J.J. is up to palling around with a ship's mechanic for an entire evening."

"So don't tell him until everything is set. Please?"

The unaccustomed plea in Cleo's voice was the clincher. "Oh, all right," Mattie relented. "Let's just hope this doesn't turn out to be a last supper for both of us!"

Cleo was ready at the stroke of eight. As if the Lord had orchestrated the plan, her father left minutes before Tom's arrival. Now she had only her mother to contend with.

When the door chimes sounded, Cleo hurried downstairs. No need to risk putting Tom through a family inquisition at the front door! She stepped back to allow the butler to open it, then offered her hand to Tom, drawing him inside.

"Hello," she greeted him, taking in the dark business suit,

the expensive cowboy boots, and the light-colored Stetson hat in his hand.

"Hello, yourself," he returned in a deep voice.

Hesitantly, she led him to the formal drawing room where her mother was entertaining a friend. "Mother, may I present Mr. Tom Kinney. Mr. Kinney, my mother, Mrs. Seachrist."

"Evening, ma'am." He nodded. "It's very nice to meet you." Cleo was surprised to see that his manner was calm and easy.

Her mother gave him a long appraising look. "Good evening, Mr. Kinney. And this is my dear friend, Mrs. Amalie Long."

"We're going out to dinner, Mother," Cleo said breathlessly. "I won't be late." She ignored her mother's quirked brow and turned to leave.

"It was nice to have met you, ladies," Tom said politely as he followed her out.

He helped Cleo into an older version of her sleek little Ford and grinned his irresistible grin. "You look absolutely smashing this evening, Miss Seachrist."

She grinned back. "So do you."

He settled himself in the driver's seat and turned the ignition key, while she noted his strong hands on the steering wheel. "I hope you won't mind," Cleo began apologetically, "but I took the liberty of asking Mattie and J.J. to join us. They'll be at her house around the corner."

"Fine with me."

She was immensely relieved. "It will be better this way, since my parents don't know you or your family."

"I wondered about that," he said, turning to her with a frown. "Perhaps we should have spent a little more time visiting with your mother and Mrs. Long," he answered smoothly.

She gave him a weak smile but offered no explanation.

"Turn here."

They went together to the door of Mattie's imposing brick home. When she and J.J. came out, Tom offered his hand to the other young man. "Tom Kinney."

"Joshua John Sagerton, III here. Known and loved by all as J.J.," he laughingly replied. "It's good to meet you."

When they entered the restaurant, Cleo did not miss the admiring looks from some of her friends as they followed Tom's progress through the crowded dining room. His manners were correct and pleasant, she observed, and he didn't appear at all out of place among them. At dinner, he sat back and let J.J. take the lead in the conversation, adding now and then a humorous anecdote of his own. Cleo thought him utterly charming.

When they excused themselves to go to the ladies' room, Mattie began to fire questions at her. "What a man! Cleo, that's no ship's mechanic! He's too smooth. Are you sure he isn't a millionaire's son in disguise? What do you know about him? Where is his home? And don't tell me Galveston. I know better than that."

"I don't know," Cleo confessed. "I haven't had a chance to talk to him alone." She wagged her finger in her friend's face. "And don't you ask him in front of everyone. I'll find out later."

When dinner was over, and Mattie and J.J. had been returned to her house, Tom and Cleo drove up in front of Cleo's door. "It's still early," she said with a smile. "And it's a lovely night. Would you like to walk a little in the garden?"

"That sounds nice."

They wandered around to the back of the house where formal paths meandered through the lush rose garden.

"Did I pass muster?" Tom asked at last, breaking their companionable silence.

"Wh—what?" Cleo was startled at his perception.

There was a knowing smile on his handsome face. "Oh, you know . . . the right clothes, the proper etiquette . . ."

She had the grace to blush lightly in the moonlight. "Why, of course, you did."

He was the one who was amused now. "But you didn't expect me to, did you? I think you should know that I wasn't always a ship's mechanic."

"Oh?" She leaned near to hear what he had to say.

"No, I grew up on a ranch in West Texas, but my mom was big on manners and polish, so I was sent away to school. Good old Mom."

"Where is your mother now?"

"Still out on the ranch. My dad died several years ago, but she won't give up ranching." He sighed. "She would have enjoyed going to dinner with us tonight. She's always loved the good life, but there's been very little of that these last few years."

"I'd like to meet her." The comment was made as a polite rejoinder, but Cleo was surprised to find that she really meant it.

"Maybe you will. I hope to get to know yours better," he added pointedly.

Again her cheeks colored in the warm night. "And *you* should know that Mother has a rather warped yardstick by which she measures people, Mr. Kinney."

"Call me Tom, and I'll call you Cleo. It's time we dropped the formality, don't you think?" Seeing her hand on the low garden wall, he covered it with his own.

"All right . . . Tom," she agreed, tasting his name in the night.

"Cleo." He lifted her hand and pressed a kiss in the palm.

A tingling sensation started in her feet and raced through her, exploding in her head as she felt his lips on her hand. Quickly regaining her composure, she withdrew it. "About my mother," she began.

"You didn't want her to know what I do for a living. Right?"

"Yes, otherwise I might not have gotten the chance to know you at all." The statement was simple and truthful. "She's not a snob, but she is inclined to be overprotective where her only daughter is concerned. Father is worse." She laughed nervously.

"And so they should be with their only treasure." He leaned back against the wall, his arms crossed casually, and observed her. "What will you do next time?"

"Next time?" She felt the tingling again.

"I hope there will be a next time," he said, looking deeply into her eyes.

In anticipation of his kiss, she leaned forward and closed her eyes. But he sidestepped her waiting lips and placed a brotherly peck on her forehead.

"I'd better get you in. No point in making your folks mad at me before they get to know me."

Her eyes flew open. And, feeling like a complete idiot, she could only nod dumbly. *I should never have allowed him to kiss me at all,* she groaned.

Walking her to the door, Tom shook her hand properly. "I'll call you again soon," he promised.

"Please do. I had a lovely evening." Dreamily, Cleo closed the door and leaned against it. "The loveliest evening ever."

Usually she called Mattie after her dates and they discussed in detail the events of the evening. But not this time. Cleo wanted to keep her feelings to herself, to sort them out, to ponder them. She fell asleep with a smile on her face.

The ringing of the phone stirred Cleo from a delicious dream, and she pulled the intrusive instrument onto the pillow.

Without cracking an eyelid, she spoke into the receiver, her voice husky with sleep. "Not now, Mattie, I'm not awake yet."

A low chuckle rumbled through the wire. "This isn't Mattie. It's Tom."

Instantly alert, she sat up in bed. "Oh, good morning!"

"I called to tell you what a wonderful time I had last night. And to see if you wanted to picnic on the beach today. Uh," he added hastily, "why don't you ask Miss Meyers and J.J. to come along, too."

It was a perfect solution to her dilemma, of course. Her mother would never permit a second encounter with this stranger without a formal meeting to check out his credentials. But as long as Cleo could say he was a friend of Mattie's and J.J.'s . . . well, seeing Tom at the beach would be a good way to avoid a confrontation with her parents before she was ready.

"Why don't we meet you at the seawall at one?" she suggested.

"Swell! I'll bring the picnic. See you later, then."

When Cleo hung up the phone, she bolted out of bed and danced around the room, giddy with excitement. It occurred to her that either the Lord was answering her prayers or she was getting herself into a terrible mess! *Either way,* she thought, *I get to see Tom Kinney again.* Then, throwing herself on the bed, she called Mattie's number.

It was impossible to keep the tremor from her voice when she had Mattie on the line. "He called again! I knew he would, but not this soon!" Cleo was bouncing on the edge of the bed, not even trying to stem her elation.

"And?"

"And we're going on a picnic today at the beach."

"You can't do that, Cleo. You're going too far this time," warned Mattie.

"Oh, it will be more or less proper . . . since you and J.J. are going with us." When there was nothing but silence on the other end, Cleo resorted to pleading. "Just one more time, Mattie. You know I never ask you for favors."

"Is it really worth all this to see him again?" Mattie hedged.

"Oh, yes! There's something about him . . . I don't know what it is, but it's never been like this with anyone before. Please . . ."

"Oh, all right. Just once more. Then you're going to have to do this the right way."

"I will, I promise! Oh, thank you, Mattie! Thank you a thousand times!"

Mattie sighed forlornly. "I hope the day doesn't come when you curse me a thousand times for aiding and abetting this insanity."

The bell at First Lutheran Church was already tolling one o'clock when they parked the car and hurried to the bathhouses. As they strolled the beach, Cleo tried not to appear to be scanning the crowd as she looked for Tom. When she finally caught sight of him, his rugged masculinity struck her again with full force. Was it the thrill of sneaking around to see him, or was he that attractive? A little of both, she truthfully decided.

"Hello," she said with studied casualness when they found him at last.

"Hello, yourself," he said, with an admiring glance at the bathing costume she had just rented. He shook hands with J.J. and acknowledged Mattie with a nod. "Miss Meyers. Nice to see you again. I have an umbrella down the beach so we can eat in the shade."

They chatted about the weather and the water as is customary when people don't know each other very well. But when they reached his chosen spot, they all settled on the blanket he had spread out on the sand.

"I'm starved! Hope the rest of you are, too." He opened the large wicker basket and passed out sandwiches and cold drinks.

"Did you make these yourself?" Mattie asked, helping Cleo place them on plates Tom had packed in the basket.

"No, there's a little place that makes great roast beef sandwiches not far from where I work. I do the barbecuing at the ranch. But outside of that, I'm not much of a cook."

While Tom distributed cold bottles of pop, Cleo searched for some lively topic of conversation to ease the awkwardness between them. Shading her eyes with her hand, she gazed out to sea. "Is that a shark out there?" she asked playfully, enjoying the sudden look of alarm on Mattie's face.

"No," said J.J. "I think it's dolphins playing. Must be six or eight of them." Then, entering into the mood, he baited Mattie, "But I heard they pulled in a two-hundred-pounder around the wharves last week."

"Had half a man's body in its stomach, so they say," said Tom with a twinkle in his eye.

Mattie's hand paused in midair, her sandwich halfway to her mouth. "You *are* just kidding . . . aren't you?"

"Yes," agreed Cleo, "they only found the man's arms."

All three laughed while Mattie shuddered. "That's not one bit funny, Cleo!" she charged. "You know that I'm deathly afraid of sharks. And I don't think any of you know a shark from a dolphin, so I have no intention of setting foot in water more than ankle-deep!"

"Then you'd better watch out for the Portuguese man of war," Tom offered solemnly. "I saw several of them while I was waiting for you."

Mattie stuck out her lip in a charming pout. "You all make the beach such a delightful place to visit."

J.J. laughed. "Don't worry, Mattie, scientists have proven that no living fish can abide a bad-tempered redhead."

She wanted to be mad, but found it impossible with her companions smiling fondly at her. And in spite of her reservations, she joined the others as they romped in the surf, but stayed as close to the shore as the tugging waves would permit.

Cleo and Tom allowed the waves to carry them out to the first sandbar. Cleo found the strength of the tide surprising as the undertow pushed and pulled her, tossing her about like a rag doll. Tom made a grab for her as she lost her footing and a wave smacked her down. He helped her to her feet as she came up, gasping for air.

They stood there, the warm water lapping at their knees, his strong arms still holding her. "The ocean plays rough," he said huskily. His eyes were intense as they searched hers.

"Yes," she whispered, hoping he wouldn't let go. She felt a tug as unmistakeable as the surf. Should she move closer . . . or farther away?

Tom sensed her indecision. "Cold?"

"A little," she admitted. They struggled in the knee-depth water toward the beach, and she allowed him to wrap her in the sandy blanket as they sat down. The sun was making a watery descent and the wind had picked up a bit.

"I could build a fire if you like," he offered.

"That would be nice." She shivered, uncertain as to whether the source of her chill was her wet suit or this disturbing man beside her.

Tom left her to pick up pieces of driftwood along the dunes, then laid a small fire in the shelter of the long salt grasses springing from the sand dune. He sat down beside her and put his arms around her lightly. She sighed as she leaned against him. "This is nice," he said.

The moon was rising over the lacy waves, casting a path of mellow light across the water. Seagulls, still circling above, cried to the sandpipers, who moved in a prissy walk at the water's edge, looking for a late supper. The sound of the water lapping against the shore had a hypnotic effect, and Cleo found herself relaxing.

"I love the water," Tom said. "Living inland, I didn't see much of it until I was in the army and was shipped overseas. But I loved it right away." He laughed softly. "I know this sounds kind of crazy, but it reminds me of the endless grassy plains I grew up with. The grass moves with the wind the same way the water does. And it makes a swishing sound as the blades rub together, a little like the sound of the waves."

"Do you have sharks, too?" she teased gently.

"Something just as deadly. Rattlesnakes."

"Oh." She shivered.

"There's some kind of danger wherever you choose to live," he reminded her. "Life is like that, you know."

Cleo pondered his words, then brightened. "I love your comparison of the ocean and the plains. I'd never thought of that. Of course, I've never seen West Texas," she admitted.

Tom shrugged. "Some people love it, some hate it. There were even stories in the early days of folks losing their minds from loneliness out on those isolated ranches."

"Is it lonely on your ranch . . . for your mother, I mean?"

"My brother Robert lives with her. And it's not that far to town."

"It must be fascinating," Cleo said, giving him a sidelong look. "I've always lived in Houston. And when we travel, we visit the large cities—Dallas . . . Austin . . . New Orleans. And I'm looking forward to spending some time in England with my family. Everyone says it's so 'civilized,' whatever that means." She laughed her low, throaty laugh. "I only know it's full of history and that it will be fun to see the places I've only read about. My father says there's even a chance we may be presented at court."

Tom frowned in thought. "That wouldn't be my choice. I'd go to the museums and art galleries. Maybe to the palace to see the changing of the guard. But I'm afraid I'd have a problem with the language."

Cleo stared in disbelief. "The language?"

"Yes. The English people I met during the war couldn't understand my West Texas twang, and I had all kinds of trouble understanding theirs. They sounded like they had a mouth full of cotton."

Cleo laughed again, liking Tom more with every new revelation.

"I hope you're not leaving anytime soon. We're just getting acquainted." His dark eyes glowed, reflecting the firelight.

"Yes, I know." She reached for his hand. "Friends?"

"Friends," he echoed solemnly. Then realizing the time, he sprang to his feet. "Hey, we'd better get back! J.J. and Mattie will be wondering where we are."

Mattie's giggle wafted across the water as they swam back to the beach and approached the fire J.J. had built to hold the gathering darkness at bay. "Hey! Is anybody home?"

"Here we are!" J.J. called cheerfully. "Come on and get warm by the fire."

Mattie gave Cleo a searching look. "We wondered if you two had sailed off the edge of the world."

"Guess we lost track of time," Cleo confessed, grateful that the night disguised her burning cheeks.

Tom dropped down beside her. "Any sandwiches left?"

"Plenty," Mattie said, fishing for them in the basket. They

made short work of them, then sat enjoying the wide sweep of moonlit beach.

"This is a swell place," J.J. said. "I'd love to have a week-end cottage out here."

Cleo chortled. "Nobody lives on the west end of the island. It's too remote."

"Oh, I don't know," said Tom reflectively. "I'd like to build a house over there so I could watch the sun go down on the water."

"Cowboys don't live on the ocean," Mattie spoke up.

Tom and Cleo exchanged knowing looks. "*This* cowboy might. I've lived long enough in the dust."

"That's what you say, but I think you must miss it some-times," Cleo added.

"What I do miss are the rodeos. I've won a few events," he said modestly.

"Where do you find the nerve to get up on one of those wild horses?" asked J.J. "That's taking your life in your hands, old man."

"Oh, J.J., *you're* scared of buildings over four stories!" scoffed Mattie.

Tom ignored her friendly jab. "I do it real carefully," he explained. "I don't mind the broncs so much, but the brahma bulls do give me the sweats. Saw a man stomped once, and I see that in my mind every time I climb aboard one. The trick is not so much staying on as getting off in one piece."

"Do you plan to work as a ship's mechanic or go back to your ranch?" J.J. wanted to know.

"Oh, I suppose I'll go back someday. Mama has things under control for now, and my brother works there since my dad died. I'm not ready to settle down yet. There's still too much I want to do and see. Grinding out my days on a ranch hasn't seemed too appealing since I've had a chance to travel with the service. It looks more like a place to *finish* things than to *begin* them."

"Most of the cattlemen who are friends of my father's have begun to look at this new oil business," J.J. said.

Tom looked thoughtful. "I've heard about it. They've found oil south of us at Pecos and Fort Stockton. A lot of money to be made, I guess, *and* to be lost. But I still hang on to my dad's old conviction: Oil and cattle don't mix."

"Well, it just may be the thing to supplement cattle and cotton here in Texas. My father's a banker and it's his business to keep up with the trends. He's already making a few loans for wildcatting," J.J. concluded.

"Got to *have* money to *make* money," Tom intoned the old saying with a grin.

"Say, Tom," J.J. said, "it might be something for you and me to consider. I wouldn't mind making a few million dollars, and you don't strike me as a man who's afraid to take a chance?"

"You and me . . . wildcat together?"

J.J. shrugged and poked up the fire. "It was just a thought. Tuck it away. There may come a time we're both ready."

Tom looked directly into the young man's eyes. He was dead serious. "Yeah, I will," he replied wonderingly.

"Just like men! Always talking business!" Cleo interrupted, getting to her feet. "Anyone for an evening swim?"

"Not me," said Mattie, speaking from within the curve of J.J.'s arm. "I'm finally warm and dry."

"Besides," said Tom, "I've heard the sharks are much worse at night." He ducked Mattie's swing and followed Cleo into the moonlit surf.

# three

Mattie peered at Cleo over her morning cup of coffee. "I'm worried about you." The statement was made calmly enough, but the expression on her face told a different story.

Carelessly Cleo twisted the china cup in her hands. "Why?" she asked, knowing the answer and the probable lecture that would follow Mattie's innocent-sounding words.

"I think you know." Mattie leaned closer to speak privately in the posh restaurant where she had met her friend for breakfast. "You've been seeing Tom for a month now, and you just can't keep sneaking around like this."

Cleo was hotly defensive. "I'm not sneaking around! We see each other openly. You ought to know! You're usually there!"

"But your parents aren't," Mattie hissed. "Why don't you take him home so they can get to know him?"

"*You* know why," moaned Cleo. "Mother would get that look on her face the minute she found out what he does for a living. And then she'd grill him on his family background. It would be awful!"

"My stars, Cleo, you've fallen for him, haven't you?" Mattie's pale blue eyes flew wide at the sudden insight. ""What on earth were you thinking?"

Cleo nodded. "I love him, Mattie. I've tried not to. I've tried to tell myself that he was just another boy. But there's something about him . . . well, I can't help myself," she finished miserably.

Mattie felt a flicker of alarm. "Surely he hasn't . . . that is, you didn't . . . let him take liberties . . .?"

Cleo blushed. "No, of course not. In fact, he's been a perfect gentleman." She laughed her throaty laugh. "Maybe that's one reason I fell for him." Her eyes took on a misty, dreamy quality. "He's so kind and thoughtful. He brought me a dozen red roses last week. . . ."

"What's new about that?" Mattie asked flatly. "Lots of boys have brought you roses."

"Yes, but Tom can't afford them. Don't you see?" Her eyes pleaded for understanding, but she didn't find it in Mattie's stony face.

"Drop him!" Mattie insisted. "Do it right away. Cut it off cleanly and forever."

"Oh, Mattie, I can't. I've tried, but I can't. I've never felt this way before."

Mattie's sigh was born of futility. "Then you have no choice but to take him home."

"If I do, Mother and Father will forbid me to see him again."

"That's because he's wrong for you," Mattie insisted.

Cleo started to protest. "He's only wrong for me by *their* standards. If he had money, everything would be all right. But I love him anyway. I'd follow him anywhere just to be with him." A tear threatened to spill down her cheek.

Mattie gritted her teeth. "You'll just have to get over it. It'll never work, and you know it. You'd be miserable. Your family would never accept him. Your father might even disinherit you! It'll never work," she repeated, then saw determination flare in Cleo's eyes. "Cleo . . ." she warned.

"Mattie, I'm not going to give him up. But you're right. I must take Tom home. They'll have to accept him. I'm their only child. Beside, they've never denied me anything I really wanted."

"Humph! You've never made such a bad choice before," Mattie reminded her mildly.

Cleo's eyes narrowed dangerously. "He's not a bad choice. He's a good and decent man. He just doesn't happen to have money. You sound like my mother!" She was shaking with anger.

"Take it easy. I only meant that socially this relationship isn't going to make anyone happy. Perhaps not even Tom," she added kindly.

"Then we'll go live somewhere else, where people will accept him for what he is."

"You'd give up everything for this man?" Mattie's eyes drilled into hers.

Cleo didn't blink. "Yes, I love him that much."

Mattie breathed a sigh of defeat. "You're either the craziest or the luckiest person I ever met. *I've* never loved anyone enough to buck my family."

Hope brightened Cleo's face. "Then you'll help me?"

"What else can I do?" wailed Mattie. "You're my best friend. But, I'm sure the Lord's going to get me for this one." In spite of her protests, Mattie was intrigued by the romantic notion of Cleo's forbidden love.

"I'll invite him over, but you and J.J. must come, too. J.J. likes Tom. Maybe that would give us a bit of an edge."

"And now you're bringing J.J. into this! Why should your parents care what he thinks of Tom?" she asked with a trace of sarcasm.

But Cleo was adamant. "I'm *not* going to let Tom get away," she said serenely. "He's the finest man I ever met."

Mattie rolled her eyes helplessly.

Cleo wiped her damp hands on a crumpled handkerchief and smoothed her hair once more. The mirror reflected a well-dressed young woman waiting for her beau to call. It failed to show how shaky that young woman felt on the inside.

Glancing at the clock, she hurried it with her eyes. *God, if you're really there, help me!*

She had prepared her parents for the meeting only by mentioning that she had invited three of her friends for tea, and that one of them was a young man. Now Henry Seachrist was reading the paper in his study, and Madeline was upstairs getting dressed. Her mother's eyebrows had risen slightly at the news, but she'd asked no further questions. After all, it was not unusual for Cleo to bring young men home for tea. It was just that this young man was not like any other she'd ever brought before, and everything depended upon the events of the next hour or so.

Wringing her hands, Cleo peered through the lacy curtains that lay beneath the heavy damask at the tall windows. Soon she saw Tom's Ford pull up in the circular drive and stop at the front door. As he stepped out, he smoothed his dark hair, and Cleo's heart gave a happy little leap.

She stepped quickly to the massive double doors as the butler opened them. "Hello, Tom. I'm so glad you could come," she said formally, her joy in seeing him mirrored in her eyes.

He took her hand. "Thank you for inviting me." He glanced over his shoulder as a second car pulled up, bringing J.J. and Mattie.

Some of the tension lifted as the four of them moved to the formal living room and chose chairs, chatting companionably. But the tension returned as her father entered the room.

The foursome rose and Cleo hurried over to greet him. Then, linking her arm through his, she led him back to the little group. "Father, I believe you know J.J. and Mattie." The two men shook hands, and Henry nodded to Mattie with a smile. But his smile faded a bit when he turned to regard Tom.

Cleo drew a deep breath. "And this is Tom Kinney."

"Happy to meet you, son." There was a wary look in Henry Seachrist's eyes as they traveled up and down the young man standing before him as if trying to place him. Or to measure him, Cleo thought. "I don't believe I've had the pleasure of meeting you. Is your family new to Houston, Mr. Kinney?" He moved easily to a chair and sat back, like a judge waiting to pass sentence.

"I don't live in Houston, sir. I live in Galveston."

Mr. Seachrist's eyes clouded a bit. "Oh," he said, quickly recovering his composure and continuing to make polite conversation. "Must be nice to live near the water."

"Yes, sir." Tom sat down again in the seat opposite his host.

At that moment Cleo's mother made a grand entrance, and the men stood as she took her place at the head of the tea table.

"You are from Galveston, Mr. Kinney? It must be dreadfully hot down there this time of year. Oh, my, and the mosquitoes!"

"What does your father do, son?" asked Mr. Seachrist as he accepted a cup of tea from his wife.

"My father is dead, sir, and my mother is back in West Texas on our ranch."

Cleo felt her stomach tighten, and her hand shook slightly as she passed the cups her mother handed her.

"A ranch," mused her mother. "How nice." Then she took on a quizzical air. "If you are a rancher, then what are you doing in Galveston?"

Cleo's throat closed. *Here it comes,* she thought.

"I work for International Shipping."

Cleo saw her mother's brow pucker slightly and her father cleared his throat.

"In their offices?" her mother asked hopefully.

"No, ma'am. I'm a ship's mechanic." Tom sat erect, his gaze calm and direct as he dropped the bomb.

Madeline stifled a slight gasp. "How nice," she repeated.

J.J. stepped in. "Mr. Kinney and I have become quite good friends." He regretted the comment the instant he uttered it, for it implied that they had been together frequently. Quickly he regrouped. "Yes, he's been quite helpful in getting Father's boat repaired. Why, we never would have figured out what was wrong with it if it hadn't been for Mr. Kinney." He glanced around the room to see if he had redeemed himself.

Cleo could see the questions still written on her father's face and took a steadying breath. "Mr. Kinney is a good friend of mine, too, Father."

Taking this as his cue, Tom stood and spoke clearly and distinctly, "Sir, ma'am, I'd like your permission to call on your daughter."

Mr. Seachrist's flinty gaze did not waver, and his voice was cool as he replied, "I don't think that would be a good idea, Mr. Kinney."

"Sir, I can see you don't approve of me, but I'm an honest man and a hard-working one. I don't intend to be working the shipyards all my life."

"Good day, Mr. Kinney. It was kind of you to call." Henry's tone carried an unmistakeable air of dismissal.

Tom remained standing, his dark eyes searching Cleo's. "Sir, I realize I have not known your daughter very long, but I love her and I think she cares for me, too. I'd like the chance to win her hand."

Cleo's heart lurched with joy. *He loves me!* It was all she heard, all that mattered.

"I'm sure you would," Mr. Seachrist replied icily. "But that won't be possible as long as I'm alive. Good day, sir."

Cleo turned a pleading look on her mother. There was

only shock and disapproval on the frozen face. "Father," she began, but he interrupted her appeal.

"You will leave now, Mr. Kinney. And you will never see my daughter again. Do you understand?" The tone he used now had subdued many a business competitor.

"I'm not going to stand here and argue with you, sir. But if Cleo will see me, I'm not going to let you keep us apart." Tom's lips thinned with determination.

Mr. Seachrist stood with his fists clenched at his sides, perhaps in an effort to keep from striking the young upstart who had defied him. Not since he was a very young man himself had anyone successfully opposed him. It was a point of pride with him that he had made his way from a position as a lowly office boy to that of the president of an international company. Yes, he had to admire the firm-jawed young man standing across the room from him, but this was different. This man had come to take his daughter away, and it was clear he was not good enough for her.

Henry's next words were as hard and cold as the iron he manufactured and shipped. "Never, never try to see my daughter again." With that, he turned on his heel and strode out of the room. Mrs. Seachrist cast a baleful eye at her daughter and followed her husband, leaving utter silence in her wake.

Cleo was almost afraid to look at Tom, but what she read in his loving gaze caused her to run to his side. He took both her hands in his. "I meant what I said to your father, Cleo. I love you, and I want to marry you." When she opened her mouth to reply, he put a silencing finger over her lips. "No, don't answer me now. Don't say anything yet. You need time to think."

"But I already know my answer, Tom," she insisted breathlessly. "I love you, too, and more than anything else in the world, I want to be your wife. I can change their minds. I know I can!"

Mattie was sobbing openly, her handkerchief stuffed against her mouth. J.J., considerably paler himself, patted her shoulder awkwardly. "Come on," he said, eager to take action. "Surely the four of us can think of something."

Mattie sighed. "Oh, J.J., you're so romantic."

The four met at the park soon after their hurried exit from the Seachrist mansion. J.J. spread out a lap rug for them to sit on, and they leaned against the ancient trees and took comfort from their shade.

Tom held Cleo's hand. "Well, you're in the soup now." His eyes searched her face for traces of regret. There was only love.

"I know. It's not the first time." She sighed heavily and glanced over at Mattie's red-rimmed eyes. "What were you bawling about back there?"

Her friend turned scarlet. "It was all so romantic the way Tom asked for your hand and then stood up to your father. Just like in the romance novels."

Tom gave a ghost of a smile. "And what would the romance novels suggest we do now?"

"We could elope," Cleo said shyly.

"No," said Tom quickly. "I think we should give your folks a little time to get over the shock. We did take them by surprise, you know."

Cleo laughed up at him. "Even *I* was surprised!" She plucked idly at his sleeve. "But I think you're right. I'll talk with them tomorrow. When they find out that I intend to marry you—with or without their blessing—they'll come around," she said confidently.

Tom laughed out loud. "Oh, you think so, do you? Are you so accustomed to having your own way? If so, I can see we have a rocky road ahead of us."

She pretended to pout. "What I meant was that when they see how much I love you, they'll give in." She reached up and, in front of J.J. and Mattie, sealed it with a kiss.

Henry and Madeline Seachrist sat in the master bedroom, each busy with thoughts too big to share. Rising, Henry paced the room angrily.

"For heaven's sake, sit down, dear." Madeline patted the satin-covered settee beside her, and he obliged.

"What do we do now?" he asked. "She left with him. She's gone."

Madeline was surprised to see the welling of tears in her husband's eyes. "She's not gone from us, Henry. She'll be back."

"Married to that fortune-hunter, no doubt," he said bitterly.

"And if the boy really loves her?"

Henry sighed. "Even if he does, how can he possibly take care of her? He's destitute—no family to speak of, no inheritance, I'll wager, and no prospects."

"We weren't rich when we got married, Henry," his wife reminded him, "and *we* managed."

"Yes, but we weren't used to all this." His sweeping gesture encompassed the luxurious room. "Cleo is. She'll be miserable with him."

"Now you can't know that, Henry. Love can compensate for many things. I *know*."

"She knows nothing of the real world out there. She's been so protected." Right before Madeline's face, grief aged his face.

She rushed to comfort him. "But what are our choices, Henry? We can never see her again, or we can accept this young man and have her back. It's possible that if she believed we would not interfere, she would drop him. You know how stubborn she is, dear . . . like her father."

A tiny light of hope crept into Henry's eyes. "You may be right. Perhaps the whole thing will die down." He stood, charged with excitement. "She'll come to her senses. If not, maybe I can give him a little incentive. There's nothing like money to change a man's mind, if that's what he's after."

"And if he loves her?"

"Oh, I have no doubt that he'll duck out when the going gets tough. Yes, Madeline, it's only a matter of time. I'll give them the biggest wedding this town has ever seen and a honeymoon in England. Then I'll offer him the job he's probably angling for anyway." He beamed, and the years fell away. "I'll scare the stuffings out of him with our way of life. He'll see he can never fit in. Yes, my dear, I believe it'll work!" He bent down and kissed his wife's forehead absentmindedly as he made plans.

It would be a wedding Houston would talk about for years. Mr. and Mrs. Seachrist opened their purse strings and dug deep. Nothing was too good for their only daughter and her new husband-to-be.

Mrs. Seachrist was in a state of near collapse by the time the day arrived, for Cleo and Tom wanted to be married as soon as possible. "Before Mother and Father change their minds!" she told Tom.

Mr. Seachrist was a bit disappointed when Tom declined his offer to work with his company, but he didn't push. Nor did he offer Tom money to call the whole thing off. No, it was increasingly apparent that the young man loved his daughter. Furthermore, where Cleo was concerned, Henry would strain all his resources to guarantee her happiness. And if this made her happy, so be it. He could wait.

For Tom, the three months before the wedding were a

nightmare of social niceties and obligations. He had asked his boss for some time off, and with a wink of understanding, the boss had granted it. It was a good thing, for Cleo had crammed his days full of fittings at the tailor, parties and dinners with her friends, and a sundry other nonessentials. He took all the activity surrrounding the wedding with consternation and a little awe. He had never seen anyone spend as much money as quickly as his bride-to-be! But she dismissed his concerns with an airy wave of her hand. "Oh, my parents want to do it, Tom, darling. Don't deprive them."

As for Cleo, she felt that when she and Tom returned from their honeymoon, he would join her father's firm and they would buy a house not too far away. Life would go on as before, but with the addition of a handsome new husband with whom to share her bliss. It was a fairy tale come true at last. Only one thing marred her joy. She suspected that her parents' dramatic change of heart about her marriage was not due to Tom's overpowering personality, but to their love for her. She had gotten what she wanted, after all, just as she had boasted to Tom she would. It was not altogether a comfortable thought, and her conscience pricked her.

Cleo was more than a little nervous at the thought of meeting Tom's family . . . especially his mother. When she confessed this to Mattie, her friend only laughed. "Oh, I'm sure it's quite the other way around. She's probably terrified of meeting *you*. After all, she's only a rancher's wife. Besides, why wouldn't she love you?"

But when Mrs. Kinney arrived for the wedding, her other son in tow, she and Cleo struck sparks on sight. A tall woman, pared down to the bone, the woman appeared to have been chiseled out of the sallow land from which she came. Under her hat, her iron-gray hair was pulled back in a severe bun. She wore no makeup and only a single gold band on her left hand.

When Cleo and her mother came downstairs, they were met by the thin-lipped woman standing ramrod-straight in their beautiful receiving room, her son slightly behind her. It was clear that he was wearing a new suit and that he was not yet comfortable in it.

Mrs. Seachrist moved gracefully to receive her guests and to put them both at ease. "Hello, Mrs. Kinney. And this must be Robert. Welcome to our home."

"Where is my son?" were the unfortunate first words from Mrs. Kinney's lips.

Madeline Seachrist ignored the tactless question and looked questioningly at her daughter. "Why, I believe he had a fitting for his morning suit, didn't he, dear?"

"Yes. He said he'd join us as soon as he was through at the tailor's."

At this, Mrs. Kinney fixed her sharp gaze on Cleo, who began to feel like a mare at auction under her future mother-in-law's intense scrutiny.

"Please sit down and I'll ring for tea," Madeline Seachrist said pleasantly, hoping to ease the awkward moments. Rarely had she met anyone with whom she couldn't form a reasonably happy relationship, no matter how brief. For Cleo's sake, she would exert all her charms on this rather unpleasant woman.

As Madeline chatted with Mrs. Kinney and her son, she made a rapid inventory of Tom's relatives. Though his mother was not dressed in style according to Houston dictates and in spite of her rude entrance, she seemed completely at ease in the opulent room. And she handled her teacup with an elegance and grace that belied her crude background. She began to wonder if Tom had not told them the entire truth about his family background. Perhaps Cleo hadn't made a mistake, after all. Good breeding always shows.

But when she and Cleo filled Mrs. Kinney in on plans for the wedding and European honeymoon, she seemed singularly unimpressed. "Waste of good money, if you ask me." Still, Madeline refused to be goaded into any kind of unpleasantness with this woman, so she chose to ignore the tart remark.

Cleo wanted very much to like Mrs. Kinney, for Tom's sake, if not for her own. *But she isn't making this any easier,* Cleo decided. And watching her mother graciously handle the difficult situation filled her with new admiration.

In spite of Mrs. Seachrist's skillful maneuvering through the rough sea of conversation, Mrs. Kinney's eyes made many a pointed reference to the gilded clock on the mantel.

"I do think Tom will be here any minute," said Cleo at last.

"I should certainly hope so," retorted Mrs. Kinney.

As if on command, Tom's handsome self appeared at the door. "Ma, Robert! It's so good to see you." He went quickly to embrace his mother and to clap Robert on the back.

"Tea, Tom?" asked Mrs. Seachrist.

"Thank you, ma'am." He accepted the delicate china teacup and, balancing it carefully, walked over to Cleo's chair. "Hello, darling, you're looking beautiful today," he greeted her, bending over to drop a kiss on her upturned mouth.

"Thank you. All done at the tailor's?"

"All done. And ready for a wedding." He grinned.

"Since you obviously intend to go through with this, son," said Mrs. Kinney who had been sullenly observing this little tableau, "I have a gift for you and your bride." With a hint of a smile hovering on her tight lips, she dug into the small bag on her lap and produced a ring. "It's my husband's grandmother's. All the Kinney men have given it to their brides. It's my wish that you wear it, Miss Seachrist." She handed the ring to Tom, who seemed perplexed, but accepted it.

"I—I don't know what to say, Mrs. Kinney," stammered Cleo when Tom had placed the ring on her finger. And truly she didn't. It was a fairly large diamond in the ugliest setting she had ever seen. She hated it, but what could she do but wear it? Swallowing her dismay, she looked up and said sweetly, "Thank you very much for the . . . ring."

Something akin to triumph glittered in the woman's eyes, but she acknowledged the comment with a nod.

When the chauffeur had at long last taken Tom and his family to the hotel and she was alone with her mother, Cleo burst into tears. "She hates me! I've never known anyone to be so mean! And just look at this ring! It's awful! Oh, Mother, how can I possibly show this thing to my friends?"

"There, there, my sweet," comforted Mrs. Seachrist, "she doesn't hate you. She doesn't even know you. Give her time." Her mother laughed softly. "You don't have to live with her. Be nice to her for the time she's here. As for the ring, we can have it reset. The stone is rather nice, and it seemed to give her great joy to give it to you. Think of it as a love gift and cherish it for that reason."

Cleo lifted her tear-stained face. "How can you be so cheerful about all this, Mother? You didn't want me to marry Tom in the first place."

"All your father and I want is your happiness, darling. I believe Tom loves you and that you love him. We can manage to do whatever else is necessary . . ." Mrs. Seachrist gave her daughter a dazzling smile, "even if it means being nice to that old battle-ax for the entire week!"

Cleo smiled through her tears. "How could someone as nice as Tom have a mother like that?" She shuddered. "At least, after the wedding she'll go home and leave us in peace.

But what have I done to make her dislike me so?"

Madeline slanted an appraising look at her daughter. "Could be she's jealous. After all, she's no longer the only woman in Tom's life."

"Were you and Father jealous, too?"

"Maybe a little, at first." She paused. "I hesitate to say this, Cleo, but if . . . well, if things don't work out the way you thought, you can always come home. Promise me you'll do that."

"I promise, Mother. But don't worry. My life with Tom will be perfect. Just wait and see."

But later, when Madeline Seachrist slipped between her satin sheets, she was deeply troubled. No matter how one looked at it, it was an unfortunate beginning.

# four

With the fairy-tale wedding and honeymoon in England only a beautiful memory, the newlyweds came home to a round of parties to welcome them to their new place in Houston society. If not a native-born son, Tom was now related to the Seachrists by marriage and therefore entitled to their civility, if not their full acceptance.

Tom went to work for Henry, the young couple found a nice old house near the Seachrists, and they settled down to begin their married life in earnest. Tom, however, was constantly amazed at the amount of money flowing out of his small bank account. He was reluctant to accept money from his in-laws, but had no choice if he was to make Cleo happy, for it was soon apparent that she had no concept of the value of a dollar. But she was happy and she made him happy, and Cleo and her parents never dreamed how often he compromised his honor to keep things that way.

Tom and Cleo spent a great deal of time with J.J. and Mattie, who were soon to be married. He liked J.J., who wasn't the typical spoiled rich man's son, but knew what it was to earn a living. His father had seen to it that he started at the bottom of the business and worked his way up. Mattie, too, was a true friend to both of them. Life was sweet . . . until the telegram.

It was from his brother Robert. "Come home immediately. Ma very sick."

Tom walked up the stairs with a heavy tread to break the news to Cleo.

"Oh, Tom, how sick is she? Is she going to die?" Cleo's

eyes filled with tears of compassion. Though she had gotten off to a poor start with Tom's mother, she knew he loved her dearly.

"I have no idea. I can't remember my mother being sick a day in her life." He looked at Cleo sadly. "I have to go to her, you know."

"Then we'll go together." Her voice was firm, despite the momentary twinge of dread.

"I can't ask you to do that. I don't know how long I might be gone."

"That's exactly why I'm going with you," she said, her tone deliberately lighthearted. "I don't want some good-looking rancher's daughter stealing you away from me!"

"But your parents . . . ."

"You come first, Tom. They'll understand. And we'll be back before you know it . . . just as soon as your mother is well again."

The train rocked and swayed, clacking briskly across the endless miles. An unusually cold November had banished any vestige of green from the barren landscape, and as Cleo looked out the window, she watched in dismay as the lushness gave way to sandy desert. Stunted mesquite stood guard over tufts of buffalo grass, dried by the ceaseless wind.

*Maybe this is what people mean by* godforsaken, she thought. She hoped not, because for the first time in her life she had the feeling she was going to need a lot of divine guidance.

"Doesn't look much like Houston, does it?" Tom glanced at her with a worried frown, acutely aware of the radical differences she would soon encounter.

Her eyes were a bit too bright when she answered him. "It's prettier in the spring, I'm sure."

"Some years," he confessed honestly. "'Course with no

rain, it's hard to tell what will happen come spring. It's been dry for nearly four years." He lifted her hand and kissed it. "I just hope you'll be happy here."

Heavy on his mind was the scene at the station. Her parents had stood, tight-lipped and mute, as Cleo had quipped about pioneering on the prairie and then kissed them good-bye with a certain bravado.

Tom had tried to prepare her for her new life, but she had remained determinedly optimistic and cheerful and simply continued to believe that "it wouldn't be for long." At her cavalier attitude, he had had grave misgivings. But he couldn't bear the thought of leaving her behind, and so was grateful for her youthful ignorance.

"Did you sleep well last night?" Tom asked.

She smiled back at him. "Like a baby. I'm so happy . . . a little scared, too. But I'm with the man I love. Whatever happens out here is the stuff family yarns are made of. We'll share them with our children." She pulled her coat more tightly around her. It was the full-length mink her parents had given her last year for her coming-out party.

Tom felt the sleek fur brush against him and remembered how he had tried to talk Cleo out of bringing it. Nothing on earth could be more inappropriate attire for life on a ranch! He feared ridicule for her. Things would be hard enough without her estranging herself from folks before they got to know her.

The coat was a vivid reminder of the first argument they'd had in their short married life, and Cleo stirred uneasily at his pointed glance. To divert his attention, she asked, "Will it be long?"

He sighed and turned to look out the window. "No. We should pull up at Monahan's Wells soon. Robert will meet us there with the wagon. Couldn't use the buggy because you brought too much stuff." His teasing tone brought the memory of another tiff. The atmosphere had been tense as they packed for their enforced farewell to civilization.

"You'll be glad I brought all that stuff someday. Just wait and see. If I hadn't brought it, you'd have had to buy it for me after I got out here," Cleo said smugly.

Tom arched a dark brow. "When we hit that sand, you'll know why the settlers littered the trails with their cast-offs all the way to California!"

Cleo regarded her husband with wondering eyes. There was much she had yet to discover about him. Memories to make together. He was like a big book she had yet to read, a new page to be explored each day. The prospect was thrilling.

Every ten miles or so, they passed a section house belonging to the railroad. These were all identically painted in yellow with black trim. The Texas and Pacific Railroad had made settlement possible in this lonely area, Tom explained. Thousands of Chinese had chopped the dry ground back and laid the rails, pushing the telegraph lines ahead of it. Wells had been dug and houses built along the double steel fingers reaching for the coast of California. The railroad was the lifeline of West Texas, a metal umbilical cord.

"Tom! What's that?" Cleo leaned closer to the open window.

"Those are the Sand Hills. Pretty, aren't they? Everyone comes out here for picnics and celebrations."

Cleo's gaze traveled over the huge shifting sand dunes, pale yellow in the late afternoon sun. The watery light revealed stubby bushes and little else. "What an odd place to party."

"What's really odd is that there are water wells all over it. Only have to dig down eighteen inches to hit the sweetest water you ever tasted. Back a ways there's a big seep pond with tall willow trees all around it. Indians have used it for no telling how long. As a boy I found plenty of arrowheads there." His eyes took on a faraway look. "Used to picnic there, slide down the dunes, chase the rabbits. It was great fun. I'll take you there first chance we get . . . when it's warmer, of course."

"Sounds a little like the beach," Cleo offered.

"Better than the beach. No sharks!" He grinned, carefully refraining from mentioning the rattlesnakes.

The train was slowing for its stop at Monahan's Wells, and they began to collect their things to get off. When they walked onto the platform, the sun was already falling behind the horizon.

"Over here!" Robert shouted. Stepping up to greet them, he embraced his brother and tipped his hat formally to his sister-in-law. "Welcome home."

Tom pounded him on the back. "It's good to see you. How's Ma?"

Robert avoided Tom's direct gaze. "Okay, I guess. She's still poorly. Hasn't left her bed for two weeks. Still don't know what's wrong with her. She won't let me get the doctor."

While the men loaded the wagon, Cleo became aware of an unbelievable stench. Robert explained that it was the holding pens, where a restless herd of cattle was confined a short distance from the platform. The cold wind carrying the foul odor had reached her nostrils and now she felt nauseous.

"You all right?" Tom asked solicitously as he took her arm to guide her to the wagon. "You look a little pale."

"Ugh!" Cleo wrinkled her nose. "I think I was just introduced to a dose of prairie perfume. A little overwhelming, but I'm fine."

Tom grinned at her and helped her into the wagon while

Robert climbed in the back to steady the boxes of supplies they had brought. "It won't be long now, honey. Can't wait to show you off to some of my friends in Kermit."

The wagon seat was not so friendly. Even with the padding of her coat, Cleo felt every jolt. The road between Monahan's Wells and Kermit, if it could be called a road, was deep sand and unexpected holes. Periodically the men got out and used shovels and hoes to dig out the sunken wheels, putting bear grass down for traction. And then there were the wire gates. Thirteen of them to open and close behind them as the horses struggled to pull the wagon through the cloying sand.

In the outskirts of Kermit, they turned off, moving in a westerly direction toward the ranch. The road there wasn't any better. In fact, it was worse, for it wasn't traveled as often.

"You're a real trouper, honey," Tom said admiringly, looking over at Cleo. "I haven't heard a word of complaint out of you the whole trip. Now, just watch for the light of the lantern."

In the growing darkness Cleo couldn't make out much of the countryside, but she could see the stars. The entire sky was ablaze with the reflection of a jillion tiny suns. "Oh, Tom, I've never seen so many stars in my whole life! And they seem so close! I do believe I could reach up and touch them. Makes me think maybe there has to be a God up there."

"Most everybody out here believes in God. Have to. We need all the help we can get just to survive."

Strange that they had never discussed it before. "Do *you* . . . believe in God, I mean?" It was suddenly very important that she know.

Tom shrugged. "I'm not much of a church going man. I like to do my meditating in the saddle. But when I'm out riding and see how everything's laid out, well, I guess we'd have to be crazy not to believe in Somebody bigger than us. Robert here's the church goer though."

"There's a church out here?" she asked, unaware until now that her brother-in-law had moved up to join them.

"Yes, ma'am. Meets every time the circuit rider comes. We have a service, singing, and dinner on the grounds." Sheepishly he added, "I look at God a different way from Tom. I believe He's there all the time, not just in an emergency."

"I'll admit He gives us the good things. But who do we blame for the bad things that happen?" Tom challenged.

"The rain falls on the good and the evil equally, the Bible says. Guess we won't know all the answers 'til we get to heaven."

Tom snorted. "I won't need them then."

"All I really know," Robert continued softly, "is that Jesus is my Savior and that He's waitin' for you to come into the flock, too, brother."

"Now, you know how I feel about sheepherders, Robert," Tom teased.

Hearing Tom's lighthearted rejoinder, Cleo felt distinctly uneasy. This whole conversation had taken a strange turn. Though she was anything but a dedicated Christian, she did have a certain respect for those who claimed to be. And now, riding underneath the canopy of brilliant stars, spangling the black velvet sky like diamonds in a jeweler's case, she was reminded that she really ought to give the matter serious consideration . . . someday.

As the wagon rolled past several windmills, the breeze playing upon their giant blades, she seized upon a safer topic of conversation. "That's a spooky sound."

"It's the sound of life out here, honey. Windmills made it possible to live in this place. I'd forgotten how quiet it can be. Guess I still have the noise of the city ringing in my ears. If you listen real carefully, you may even hear a coyote singing of a lost love."

She glanced about, her eyes wide. "There really are coyotes out here? I thought that was just in western stories."

"Honey, that's where you are," Tom explained patiently. "The West. The frontier. Oh, someday we'll catch up with the rest of the world. We just need a little time."

"And rain," Robert put in. "Haven't had a good rain in so long the rattlers have been knockin' on the door for a drink."

"You are joking, aren't you?" Cleo shivered as she tried to read her new brother-in-law's expression in the starlight.

"No point in scaring her to death before she gets there, Robert," Tom said mildly.

"Sorry, Cleo," said Robert. "Don't worry, rattlers sleep in the winter. You won't have to watch out for them . . . except on warm days . . . 'til spring."

She grinned at Tom weakly. "I *think* that makes me feel a lot better."

Despite the bumping of the wagon, Cleo found herself drowsing against Tom's shoulder. So she had no sense of how much time had passed when he finally roused her. "Wake up, Cleo. There it is."

She opened her eyes, but saw nothing except the darkness, thick as a quilt, stretching before them. "Where?"

"See that little light over there? That's the lantern on the windmill. Ma must've hung it out."

In the pale starlight Cleo could see the outline of a tall windmill, standing like a sentinel over a small house. The lantern's unblinking eye guided their approach.

Cleo fought off the feeling of despair as she made out the contours of a tiny house. As they neared, the door opened and a small figure stood silhouetted in the light that spilled out into the night.

"There's Ma," Robert said. "She must be feeling better."

Cleo was cheered by this news. Maybe their visit would be even shorter than she'd hoped.

They pulled up in front of the house, and Tom helped Cleo down. He took off his Stetson as he embraced his mother. "Hello, Ma."

"Hello, son. I'm glad you're home. We been needin' ya around here."

Cleo saw Robert duck his head and turn away. Since no one seemed inclined to acknowledge her presence, Cleo stepped up to greet her mother-in-law, who was in her nightclothes, a large shawl pulled around her frail figure. "Hello again."

The woman made no attempt to embrace her daughter-in-law, but merely nodded. Her voice was firm and tinged with a heavier rural accent than Cleo remembered as she said, "Hope your trip wasn't too hard on ya."

"No, it was quite pleasant. An adventure, really."

"Well, come on in. The boys can git your things." She led the way into the house. "Robert, fetch the lantern off the windmill."

Buttery soft lamplight softened the austerity of the room, half of which served as a kitchen and the other half as living quarters. Cleo lowered herself onto a well-worn sofa and looked around. It was a practical room, with odd touches of culture. A leather-bound set of the classics, obviously handled by many loving hands, stood in the bookcase.

"Would you like a cup of coffee, or do you just want to go on to bed?"

Not knowing whom Mrs. Kinney was addressing, Cleo turned to Tom for guidance.

"I think we'll go on to bed, Ma," he said, "We're all beat. There'll be time to talk in the morning."

As Mrs. Kinney turned for her bedroom, she said, "You

can have your old room, Tom.  Robert can sleep in here."

Cleo felt a twinge of guilt, knowing they had pushed Robert out of his room, and tried to communicate her appreciation with a smile.  But she was to exhausted to argue.  Obediently she followed Tom to their new bedroom.

"This is it," he said, seeing the spartan surroundings through Cleo's eyes.  "You all right, honey?  You look a little pale."

"I'm tired, that's all."  She smiled at the worried look on his face.  "I'll be fine after a good night's sleep."

When she surveyed the sagging bed with its patchwork quilt, even that prospect seemed doubtful.  And long after Tom lay sleeping, she was still awake, pondering the enormity of this change in her life.  As much as she loved her husband, would she be able to adjust to his world?  The thought was heavy on her mind as she slipped into a troubled sleep.

The aroma of frying bacon and hot coffee beckoned Cleo from the warmth of her nest beside Tom.

"Morning, sleepyhead," he said softly and pulled her back against him.  His face looked relaxed and loving in the morning light.

"I'll cuddle later.  Right now I need to step into the bathroom," she said with modesty.

He grinned wickedly.  "Then you'd better wear that fur coat.  The privy is down by the barn."

"Oh, no!  Tom, are you serious?"

"Never more serious.  It's at the back of the house," he said and ducked the pillow strategically aimed at his head.

Cleo threw him a dirty look and wrapped a warm fluffy robe about her, then hurried down the outside path.  "Now this is ridiculous," she mumbled to herself as she opened the wooden door and peered in.  Never having seen a privy in her life, she was amused at the quaint single hole carved into the wooden bench. But the iciness of the seat sent a shock wave up her spine.

She thought of her luxurious quarters back home—the spacious bedroom with private bath—and gritted her teeth. *It'll only be for a little while,* she reminded herself.

Cleo had almost made it back to the house when she ran into Robert. Unable to hide her embarrassment, she blushed furiously. "Oh, good morning!"

Robert's own ruddy complexion deepened when he spotted Cleo in her nightclothes, and he did the only thing a Texas gentleman could do under the circumstances. He tipped his hat and moved on silently.

Tom was pulling on a pair of well-worn boots when Cleo returned. "Why don't you get dressed, honey, and after breakfast we'll go riding and I'll show you around?"

"Do I have time for a quick bath first?" She was eager to remove the grime from the train ride the day before and had noticed a metal tub standing in a small cubicle at the rear of the house when she'd passed by on her way to the privy.

"A very quick one. But," he paused, hesitating to tell her this news, "you need to know . . ."

"Yes, Tom?" She turned to him with a bright smile.

"There isn't any running hot water. It'll have to be heated. But I can put on a kettle if you like."

The idea that he was joking died quickly. "I'll help you. Guess I'd better learn everything right away," she said on a positive note.

As they entered the kitchen, Mrs. Kinney was busy at the stove. She made no comment when Tom got out the two big pots, filled them with water at the kitchen sink, and put them on the back burners of the wood-burning stove. "Mornin'," she said not looking up.

"Good morning," Cleo replied and beat a hasty retreat to

the privacy of their bedroom, not quite ready to begin the day with Mrs. Kinney.

When at last the tub was half-filled, she added some cold water from the tap and stepped in gingerly. Opening her little travel bag, she got out the soap she had brought, eyeing with horror the lye soap on the little shelf over the tub.

When she drained the tub after her bath, she saw a fine netting of red sand left in the bottom. *I could have scrubbed myself without the soap,* she thought.

Hastily she put on a split skirt, a silk blouse, and her English riding boots, feeling more like herself than at any time since she'd left home. Funny how a night's sleep and a good bath changed one's perspective, she thought, combing her hair and pulling on the black derby hat she always wore when riding. With a final satisfied look in the mirror, she made her way back to the kitchen.

"Good morning again," she said cheerfully as she paused at the door. "The bacon and coffee smell divine."

Tom was frankly admiring as she took her place beside him at the table. "You look as fresh as a prairie dawn," he said.

She *felt* more like a prize mare at a stock show as the three of them stared at her. Mrs. Kinney was dressed in a faded cotton skirt that reached her ankles. An apron covered most of her front. Cleo knew at once that she herself was overdressed, but these were the most casual riding clothes she owned. She smiled her thanks at her husband, then accepted the mug of hot coffee Mrs. Kinney handed her.

Cleo's gaze traveled around the plain room. In the daylight, she could more clearly see the wooden cupboards, some missing their knobs, gaping open above the worn cabinets. An old cookie jar, shaped like a fat man, stood on the side of the cabinet next to the wood-burning stove. At least,

Cleo thought, the room was clean and felt homey. She began to relax.

"How do you want your eggs?" Mrs. Kinney asked.

"However you're preparing them will be fine." Cleo had vowed to do everything possible to get along with this strange woman while she was under her roof, but she did hate eggs with runny centers.

The pale yellow yolks quivered as Mrs. Kinney set the plate in front of her, but Cleo bravely tasted the fare. "Mmm, these preserves are wonderful," said truthfully.

Tom glanced at her with a grin. "We get the plums from a thicket in the Sand Hills every summer. It's a big family affair, and most everybody joins in. Of course, Ma makes the best preserves in the county."

"You always did have a sweet tongue, Tom," Mrs. Kinney protested, but she couldn't hide the pleasure in her voice.

She had prepared a huge breakfast of bacon, eggs, biscuits, gravy, small beef steaks, and coffee. "You boys eat hearty now," she urged, "there's a lot of work to be done today. It's good to have you home, son. We've missed ya."

Mrs. Kinney sat down at the table, but ate sparingly of the meal. "Need to check on the stock out in the east pasture. They may need some extra feed. No rain, no grass, so they're gettin' mighty hungry by now. There's cottonseed cakes in the barn, Tom. You and Robert can load the wagon."

She was preparing to list the rest of the chores when Tom cut in. "Wait, Ma. I want to know what's going on here." He leveled her a penetrating look. "First, I hear you're deathly sick. Then I come home to find you on your feet. Just why *did* you call for me?"

"Druther not talk family business right now," she said testily, eyeing Cleo.

Tom bridled. "Cleo is my wife, Ma. That makes her part of the family. And she's entitled to your courtesy as well as your hospitality."

There was stunned silence around the table before Mrs. Kinney replied. "'Course she is, son," she said in a conciliatory tone. "Just didn't think her first meal was the time to be talkin' about hard times, that's all."

Tom considered her answer, studying her expression. He couldn't tell if she were patronizing him or not. Rarely had he been able to read his mother's face, for she had always kept her emotions carefully hidden away from prying eyes.

"I came home to find out what's going on," he said quietly. "I left a good paying job, my new home, and our way of life. If I'm not needed here, then I'll get back to that life."

"All right, son. I'll lay it out for ya," said Mrs. Kinney. "We're late with the payments on the ranch, and the bank is trying to foreclose on us."

Tom let out a long whistle. "Land-rich and cash-poor. The code of the rancher," he said grimly.

"Yep." A sad smile barely reached Mrs. Kinney's eyes.

"What's the bank going to do with all this land? Things are so bad there's no way they can sell it."

Mrs. Kinney took a sip of her coffee. "Seems like they've discovered oil down by Pecos. Old Kirby's got the itch. Buyin' up all the land he can get his hands on."

"But Pecos is seventy-five miles away. What does that have to do with us?"

"They struck in Ranger, too, and we're sittin' smack-dab between."

"There's no oil out here, Ma," Tom insisted. "People have already looked for it. Kirby's just whistling Dixie. Why, there's barely a rise for fifty miles. How can there be oil?"

"Probably isn't, but Kirby is buyin' up the land anyway. And leasin' what he can't buy. That's not our problem. Money is." Cleo looked at Tom's stricken face and kept silent.

"I'll go talk to him tomorrow. Maybe I can get an extension." He smiled wanly. "Meanwhile, we'll knock out some of the work that's been piling up around here. How many hands you got working now, Ma?"

"Just three. They're hard workers, but they don't know a whole lot about ranching. They need a strong hand behind them."

Robert blushed deeply.

"I know you do your best, son," said Mrs. Kinney, noting her younger son's embarrassment, "but they need someone who won't be timid about tellin' them what to do and when to do it. With things so bad, I don't have the heart to fire 'em. They have families, too."

Cleo could see the new resolve as Tom flexed his jaw. "Robert and I will see to things, Ma. Don't worry."

"Just so you know. I *have* been sick. Sick at heart, I guess. I've been through this so many times . . . don't think I've got the strength to fight it again. Not without your pa."

Tom placed his hand over his mother's work-worn one.

There was a hint of tears in the woman's eyes. "We'll make out, son, now that you're here. Now get out of here and get to work."

Tom rose from the table and squared his shoulders. "Come on, Cleo. You can find out what a real cowboy does on a ranch."

"Better put on something warm to wear over them clothes," counseled Mrs. Kinney. "But not that mink coat. It would set us back a ways if the banker was to see it."

Cleo felt the sting of the waspish tongue, and Tom answered instead. "Now, Ma, don't you go trying to sell that coat while we're gone. Or wear it, either," he said in an attempt to lighten the mood of the past few moments.

"Humpph," was her only reply to his needling.

As they walked to the corral, Cleo thought about the diamond ring Mrs. Kinney had given her. Her mother-in-law could have sold that ring and used the money to pay off the mortgage on the ranch. Suddenly it took on new value for Cleo. She'd keep the ring and never have it reset. It was a family heirloom she meant to pass on to her children, along with the story of their grandmother's sacrifice.

"What are you going to do now, Tom?" she asked softly as he saddled the horses.

"Work today. Talk tomorrow." He held her horse as she swung up into the saddle. "Let's just take one day at a time."

She nodded meekly. She wanted to talk about money. Her father's money. But it could wait . . . until tomorrow.

## five

In the space of a morning's ride, Cleo was alternately shocked, dismayed, enthralled, and disappointed in the Texas landscape. The trackless land rolled on for miles, broken only by an occasional rise. There were stunted mesquite trees and cold-shocked cactus and patches of dried grass that ran haphazardly across the vast prairie.

From Tom, Cleo learned that the land had been carved out by only two elements—the constant wind and extreme temperatures—for water had not touched this desolate stretch of country in a very long time. In places, the wind had eroded a corner of a rise, exposing the red earth under the ratted prairie grass that competed for breathing space. The surface was truly red. The varicolored layers of earth beneath could be seen like the layers of a cake.

"Does it ever snow out here?" Cleo asked, huddling into the heavy leather jacket Tom had brought out for her. Behind them, Robert rattled along in the wagon that held cottonseed cakes for the cows.

"Once a year. In February." Tom squinted from beneath his hat as he scanned the horizon. What he saw—the vast nothingness—was a balm to his spirit. Houston and Galveston bustled with busyness, with people rushing about madly, hurrying to work, hurrying to have fun. Here all was relatively serene.

The furrow returned to his brow when he thought about his mother's revelation at breakfast. There was never enough cash to go around. What little came in from cattle sales had to be plowed back into improving the herd or making needed repairs around the place. Land was sacred to a rancher, something to be worked and held onto at all costs. Tom's optimism had been intended to encourage his mother, but the truth was that he was as worried about the money as she. Losing the ranch would finish her off, would end his dreams, too. The ranch was everything—their roots, their inheritance to be passed on to their children and grandchildren. He had dreamed of building an empire like his father before him. He had temporarily abandoned the dream in a young man's pursuit of adventure, only to return and find it more precious than he could have ever imagined.

Well, Tom Kinney was back, and he intended to fight for his dream. He had a lovely young woman by his side, one who loved him more than he deserved. Their months in Houston had been a shallow sojourn, a way of life he knew now he could never have truly embraced. Now, for the first time in years, he felt a vital new excitement throbbing in his veins.

He shifted in the saddle and turned to Cleo. Seeing her in the bright November sunlight only heightened his joy and his resolve. He would save the ranch, not just for his mother, but for Cleo . . . and their children!

"Beautiful, isn't it?" he exulted, caught up in the grandeur of his vision.

"It—it's so . . . *big*," she breathed, trying hard to find the beauty he was seeing. "Where are the cattle?"

"Out in the east section. There's better grass there . . . what there is of it. Before I left, it was pretty decent. Now things are looking mighty dry."

"Is there a lake or something out there?"

Tom laughed. "No, something more dependable. Windmills, remember? That old Eclipse near the house has been pumping water forever. Pa had it brought in when he first claimed this land. The water isn't far down. Just have to find it. Indians knew all the natural wells, but we've made our own. When people travel on horseback, they keep their bearings by using the windmills as landmarks. Each one is as individual as a horse with its own peculiar sound."

"How do you know where to look for the water?"

"Found ours by using a peach branch fork." He laughed at the look of disbelief on her face. "Amazing thing."

"Maybe you could find oil that way, too."

Tom's face clouded. "I don't want to find oil. We don't need that stuff out here. This is cattle country."

"I'm sorry. I only meant to make a joke," she apologized lamely.

He flashed her a grin. "Guess you hit a nerve. Just remember to keep your priorities straight. Out here, cows come first."

"Ahead of people?"

Tom flexed a muscle in his jaw. "A man can only hope he never has to make that choice."

They rode in silence for a time until the tension eased while Cleo tried to bridge the distance between them. Just then she spotted the cattle, moving like a colony of insects across an endless ocean of space. As they neared, the animals ambled toward them, anticipating the food. The men scattered the seedcakes from the wagon, dropping them in a long line to string out the hungry cows.

"Oh, Tom, they're beautiful. They're the same color as the dirt, all red rust. And their little white faces . . ." Cleo watched as the cattle began to eat, lowing in contentment. But she was grateful that the wind was blowing in the opposite direction!

A dream spider wound a silken web of unreality around her as she looked on. Could she really be here in this place, seeing these things with her own eyes? Her husband—a cattleman? Only a short while ago, she had thought him some rich man's son on holiday as she'd watched him at play in the blue waters of the Gulf.

Was she also poor now that she was married to a poor man? She still had all her family's resources at her fingertips, but if she lived on what her new husband could provide for her, wouldn't that make her poor? A quick stab of disloyalty pierced her. *I love him, no matter what,* she thought stubbornly. And though everything was still new, she had the feeling she had belonged to Tom all her life and that eternity was just beginning.

That night in the privacy of their bedroom, Cleo tried to approach Tom about their financial plight. She had thought about it off and on all day as they rode around the ranch. Instinctively she knew that his male pride was involved, and she tried to be tactful.

"Darling, I know how much the ranch means to you, especially now that I've seen it for myself." She trailed a caressing finger across his cheek as they lay in bed. "Please let me write to Father. . . ."

But that was as far as she got before he turned on her in fury. "This is *my* world! Your father's money has nothing to do with my ranch." Seeing the shock on her face, he relented. "I'm sorry, honey, I didn't mean to yell at you, but out here I'm my own man," he continued with great earnestness. "Your family has been good to me—the wedding, the house, the job—but we both know they did it for you. Out here, I have to do things my way. I can't depend on your father's money to help me out of every problem I face from now on. Do you understand what I'm saying?"

She was trying to. "Has it been that difficult for you?" Her words were tinged with anger and hurt.

"Sometimes," he admitted. "But I wanted you to be happy, and I knew I couldn't give you all those things. Not right away." He sighed. "Things are different now, Cleo. Now you live in my world. It's not what you've been used to, but it's mine, it's what I have to give. I hope it's enough."

He wrapped his arms around her, pulling her close and inhaling the fragrance of her hair against his face. "I love you, and I promise you'll never do without the most important things. I may not be able to give you luxuries, but I can make you happy. Trust me. Let me do it my way. At my own pace. In a few years this ranch could be one of the best in the state. I know it."

Cleo was still, absorbing the impact of his words. "You're saying it would spoil things if I got the money for you?"

"Something like that. All I'm asking for is a little more time. Can you give it to me?"

At the look of pleading in his eyes, there was nothing to do but go along with him. "All right," she agreed quietly. "We'll do it your way. But if the time ever comes . . ." The rest of her words were closed off by the pressure of his lips on hers.

*This is all I really need,* she thought. *His love is enough. Everything else can wait.*


The next morning Cleo endured the ritual of a lukewarm bath in a cold room, for this was the day they were going to town to see the banker.

Before breakfast, she dressed with care, putting on a kelly green morning dress from her trousseau and adjusting her stockings. Pulling on a green cloche over her dark hair, she took a final look in the mirror and smiled at her reflection. This outfit always made her feel attractive and feminine.

Hurrying into the other room, where Tom and the others were already seated, Cleo took her place at the table. "Good morning."

There were mumbled greetings and a great deal of

shuffling around the table.

Cleo looked up in surprise. "Is something wrong?"

"Honey," began Tom in a strained voice, "you can't go to the bank dressed like that. They'd laugh in my face."

"On the contrary. You know what Father always said: It takes money to make money. Bankers don't want to lend money to people who don't look as if they can pay them back, do they?" She arched her thin brows.

The brothers exchanged a look of confusion. "Maybe not in Houston," Tom spoke up, "but out here, it makes the bankers feel righteous to give money to down-and-outers."

"Hey, Tom," said Robert slowly, "why not give 'em the Houston treatment? It just might work."

Tom chewed on a biscuit as he turned it over in his mind. "It just might," he echoed, grinning. "I'll change and be right with you, honey."

Cleo tried to make small talk with Mrs. Kinney and Robert while she waited, but it all sounded so silly. She was enormously relieved when Tom came back, dressed in his best suit and his good boots. "You look mighty handsome, sir," she said, noting that the boots and the Stetson were a perfect complement to his rugged good looks.

"Why thank ya, ma'am," he drawled in an exaggerated voice.

Cleo had noted the distinction between Tom's softer speech and his family's country dialect, believing that it could be attributed to his time in the service and the desire to wash away the sand of the ranch. Since being home, however, he had occasionally lapsed into that familiar dialect. Right now, for example, she found it charming.

"Ready?" he asked as he pulled on the soft gray hat.

Cleo gathered up her purse and gloves. "Ready."

"Don't forget the coat," was Mrs. Kinney's only parting remark.

Tom helped Cleo into the mink. "If this doesn't impress them, nothing will." He eyed the strand of pearls around her neck. "You don't have a big chunk of diamonds stashed away somewhere, do you?"

She smiled up at him and flashed the diamond ring his mother had given her. "Will this do?" She was moved to see a sheen of tears in the woman's eyes.

On the way to town, Tom had to stop several times to dig the carriage wheels out of the sand. Cleo sat on the seat, feeling the tug of unreality once more, and her mind wandered. *Here I am,* she thought, *in the middle of nowhere, stuck in the sand with a man I didn't even know six months ago, riding in a buggy to see a banker who can take away a ranch I don't care about from a woman who has been less than friendly to me. What am I doing here?*

But when Tom climbed in beside her again, she knew. "We'll get there," he assured her. "'Course it might be next year."

She reached for his arm, tucking her hand through it, and snuggled close. His nearness, the familiar tangy smell of him was reassuring. She smiled at him and they rolled on for several miles in companionable silence.

At last Cleo broke the silence. "What am I going to do about your mother?" she asked softly.

Tom clenched his jaw. "Just . . . wait. She'll come around. No one could resist you for very long."

But Cleo was not convinced. "I don't think I ever met anyone who disliked me so much and let me know it. At least, the people in Houston are more subtle." She smiled sadly. "She won't even give me a chance."

"I know Ma. She'll come around." Tom forced a hearty tone, then he frowned. "She acted so nice at the wedding. I honestly thought things were going to be all right. Guess she had me fooled. Ma is strange. Living out here alone can do that to a person." He slipped his arm around her and squeezed hard. "You're more woman than she's used to coping with. Give her time."

*But how much time?* Cleo wondered. She had hoped to be back home in Houston to see the first daffodils. But now it appeared that Tom had other ideas.

She fought off the biting cold and eyed the desolation that stretched endlessly before them. Though they were traveling down the same road that had brought them here only a few hours ago, everything looked strangely unfamiliar. It was disconcerting to see the same scenery over and over with nothing distinctive to mark its passage. "Tom, how on earth do the the cows survive out here?"

He shrugged. "They're tough. It takes a lot of land to support one cow. That's why we need so much of it. But in the spring this prairie will green out and if we get some rain, there will be plenty of grass. We'll round up the cattle and see who survived the cold and the coyotes. Brand the new calves. Save the best and move some to market for cash to operate on. It's not a bad life, really."

"Sounds like you sit back while the cows and bulls do all the work."

Tom flicked the reins to encourage the horse over a deep rut. "Come roundup time, you'll see. It's the hardest job I've ever done. And I've done some hard labor in my time." His eyes took on a faraway look. "It's a sight to behold. Men yelling and whistling. Cows calling to their calves, and the calves bellowing when the hot iron hits them. Bulls objecting to the slice of the knife. And sand. By gum, I think half my body is made up of sand!"

Cleo could not resist his little-boy look of pleasure. "And you love every minute of it! It's written all over your face." She felt herself longing to share more of his life, to understand his love for this land. A roundup sounded like fun. "Maybe we could have a barbecue in the spring after the roundup and invite Mattie and J.J. and my parents. . . ."

Spring. It sounded like forever. But maybe she could make it that long. Besides, she was confident Tom would be ready to get back to civilization as soon as he was sure the ranch was safe and operating in the black again.

"Let's take one thing at a time," he said, looking grim. "First, we go to the bank to do battle with the money-grubbing ogre who wants to cancel the whole deal."

Tom had no idea what the bank's reaction would be, for no one in the county had seen anyone like Cleo. But then the element of surprise was always useful during a fight, he thought with satisfaction.

"There it is. Wink," Tom said, gazing off into the distance. "Now don't expect too much," he warned.

Spread out ahead was the little town of Wink—all six buildings!

"There's the bank, of course," Tom pointed out as they rumbled into town. "The post office is in the general store, owned and operated by Mr. Blankenship and his wife. Slick Slattery owns the machine shop in town. And Mrs. Court has a house and lets out a room to Slick." He gestured toward a barn. "That's the livery stable over there. Blankenship's son takes care of it when there's any business. And down there is old Kirby's house." It was a nice home, with flowers planted and carefully tended in front of the little white picket fence. He shrugged. "That's all there is."

Cleo could feel Tom's tension as he pointed out the landmarks. Whether it was brought on by dread over their errand or by his desire that she approve, Cleo could not decide. "It's all so . . . quaint. You have everything you need here." She couldn't lie, but she didn't want to hurt his feelings either, and she thought she saw worry cloud his eyes as they made their way down the heavily rutted dirt street toward the bank.

It was not an impressive building, but it appeared solid. Built of red brick, the bank was fronted by a small porch supported by white columns.

Cleo took Tom's hand as she stepped from the carriage. A chill wind fanned her cheeks and ruffled her hair and she pulled the coat more snugly around her.

Tom smiled down at her. "Ready?"

She took a steadying breath. "I think so."

The big smile she flashed him bolstered his courage, and Tom squared his shoulders to face the man who could wipe him out and end all their dreams.

He chose not to remove his gray Stetson inside the building, feeling that to do so would lessen his stature. He simply couldn't enter the bank, hat in hand. He needed an edge. His manner, along with his expensively dressed wife, just might get him the money he so desperately needed.

"Hello, Leaf," he greeted the young woman sitting at the front desk.

She was petite and attractive, Cleo thought, and could have been beautiful if she had known how to use the many beauty aids Cleo had packed in her little traveling bag. Cleo liked her immediately, but felt a bit of pity for this young person trapped in this little spot in the road. She gave Leaf her warmest smile.

"Leaf, this is my wife, Cleo."

Leaf studied her openly, visually caressing Cleo's mink coat and fine clothes. "Why, I'd heard you got married, Tom." Not taking her eyes off Cleo, she rose gracefully and walked toward them, extending her hand. "Hello. Welcome to Wink."

Her eyes were a bit too bright and the smile held a note of

falsity, but Cleo took her hand. "It's very nice to meet you. I could use a new friend so far from home."

"It does get a little lonely out here sometimes," admitted Leaf before she turned a warm smile on Tom. "I know Papa will be glad to see you, Tom. He talks about you a lot."

Tom laughed. "I'll just bet he does! Probably talks about me behind my back for leaving the ranch, doesn't he?"

Leaf laughed, a high tinkling sound. "Matter of fact, he does. He never did understand about that. But some of us did."

At the look Leaf gave Tom—hungry, sad, defeated—Cleo knew. Leaf was in love with her husband! The thought struck her like a bolt of lightning, and for a brief second, she was frightened.

But in the next instant, she had all the reassurance she needed.

"My wife and I would like to see your father, please," Tom said pointedly, taking Cleo's hand and tucking it possessively through his arm.

*So he knows Leaf is in love with him,* thought Cleo. There was no time to dwell on this discovery before she and Tom were ushered into Mr. Kirby's office.

The room was small by Texas standards and sparsely furnished. But there was no mistaking the western decor. A stuffed longhorn cow's head hung on one wall, and the other walls appeared to have been marked with various brands, perhaps burned into the wood with branding irons, Cleo guessed. But it was the glass case standing on a table that made her blood run cold. On display was a live rattlesnake, coiled inside a cow's skull.

"You're safe, madam. Felix is sealed up real tight."

The room was pungent with cigar smoke that hovered in a visible cloud around the speaker. The man had stood to his feet and was moving briskly to greet them, dangling his cigar in one hand and extending the other for Tom's handshake.

The portly executive was wearing a suit, Cleo noted right away, the fine material stretched taut across an impressive bay window where a watchchain swung importantly. He had a full head of very white hair, and his eyebrows were wild and free as they roamed fiercely across his forehead. Sharp, snapping eyes took in every detail of her expensive attire as the banker took Cleo's hand and led her to an overstuffed chair opposite his desk.

Here was a man to be reckoned with, Cleo thought. She'd met his kind before, though never in a business transaction, of course. She listened carefully as the two men observed the rituals of greeting.

"Heard you'd got hitched, Tom. Appears you did quite well for yourself. She's a looker."

Cleo felt an undeniable spark of anger. This was the second time she had heard herself referred to as if she were not even in the room. It rankled her.

"Yeh, heard you married a Houston girl. Bet she finds West Texas a big surprise. Your ma doin' better?"

"She's still a bit off her feed, but she'll be good as new in no time." Tom sat down beside Cleo, and Mr. Kirby eased his ample girth into the chair behind his desk.

"Guess I know why you're here, Tom. Sorry about your financial embarrassment. Sorry, too, about the ranch . . . ."

Cleo had never heard such a lie! The cold blue eyes, in stark contrast to the thin-lipped remark, registered not one whit of sympathy.

"No need to feel sorry. We're here to settle that matter right now," Tom said smoothly. "Of course, my money is back in Houston, so if you'll let me sign a personal note until I can liquidate some of my holdings back there, we'll be in business."

Cleo was fascinated. Tom had never mentioned any "holdings." They'd tried to live on his salary, but when that hadn't covered her expenditures, her father had picked up the bills. She blushed, realizing the burden she must have been.

"What kind of holdings are we talkin' 'bout?" Kirby's narrow-eyed gaze reminded Cleo of a dangerous animal who had been cornered, but not yet captured.

"Real estate mostly," Tom replied with a bland expression on his face. "Of course, there's my wife's jewelry, our home, the cars we left behind. . . . "

Admiration and fear charged through Cleo. Would the banker be impressed?

Kirby chewed on this information briefly, then conceded defeat. "You've done good for yourself, Tom. 'Course, I'll accept your word and arrange the loan. It's been nice doin' bidness with you." Kirby seemed gracious enough, but Cleo knew he'd always be around, waiting for a chance to gobble up another ranch. He was not a man to be trifled with, and she hoped they wouldn't have to do "bidness" with him again.

"Nice to meet you, Mrs. Kinney. I'll draw up the papers right away, Tom. You can pick 'em up before you leave town."

Tom nodded. "We'll be at the general store, buying a few things we need." He rose and shook the flabby hand again.

"You were very convincing back there, Tom," Cleo said outside the bank as they were climbing into the buggy.

He grinned broadly. "You weren't bad yourself, Mrs. Kinney." The name still sounded strange in her ears. "But I learned something today. I learned that you can do what you set your mind to. Imagine me, walking in there to old Kirby and coming out with the money I need." His countenance was glowing. "You're the best collateral I ever had, honey." Then he sobered. "Now all I have to do is get the money to pay off Kirby and keep him off my back."

"What will you do when the loan comes due?" she ventured.

"Whatever I have to," he said grimly. "My grandpa fought Indians, my Pa fought the drought and squatters, and now I'll take on old Kirby to keep this land."

The intensity of Tom's declaration frightened Cleo, for it sounded like he anticipated a long-drawn-out battle. Her thoughts roiled. *Tom is so happy here. He's his own boss, not Father's son-in-law. But if we stay much longer, we'll never get out of here!* Her mind spun, seeking an answer to her dilemma. Would she ever be able to persuade her husband to return to Houston?

*Please, God, don't leave me out here in this strange land,* she prayed. *Help us get home. And show me how to make Tom happy.*

There was no one else to whom she could turn. Maybe this wasn't a forsaken land, after all. Maybe God would hear her cry for help. But time would tell if He heard prayers, even in West Texas.

## six

Cleo stood out in the cold air behind the privy, throwing up as quietly and delicately as possible. As she leaned against the rough wood frame, she blamed her husband and then she blamed herself for this carelessness. She took a deep breath of the cool air to settle her stomach, but the acrid smell hit her nostrils instead, and she threw up again as she clung to the little house for support.

She had been replaying this scene for a whole week, so there was no doubt in Cleo's mind that she was pregnant. But the thought of having a baby out here without her parents to help her struck terror to her heart. She longed for her mother's sheltering arms, and her father's assurances that everything would be fine.

Instead, she had a mother-in-law who was barely civil and a husband who expected her to drop the baby as easily as the cows out in the pasture. He, of course, was absolutely delighted. Proof of his masculinity and prowess, she thought bitterly. She felt every inch the victim.

When her stomach calmed down enough for her to return to the house, Cleo walked back to the bedroom and stretched out on the bed, fully clothed. She heard the door open softly.

"Feeling better?" Tom asked hopefully, feeling a little guilty that she was so sick. She looked so fragile and pale lying there. "Can I get you anything?"

"A little weak tea would be nice. And a piece of dry toast," she mumbled.

Tom's mother was in the kitchen when he went in to heat the water. He stuck a few more pieces of mesquite in the stove.

"Is she still feeling poorly?" Mrs. Kinney wanted to know.

"Yes."

"I know how she feels, believe me. But," she said a bit smugly, "*my* husband didn't wait on *me*. We were too busy trying to make a go of this place. I just toughed it out by myself. And that's when there was still Indian trouble in these parts."

"Ma, you know the Indians hadn't raided for years before you were expecting me," Tom chided.

"Now, son, you don't know what you're talking about. There were still a few renegades about." She gave him a challenging look and shoved a roast in the hot oven.

Tom refused to be drawn into another argument with his mother. As time went by, she seemed to grow harder and more unyielding, but he must not let Cleo bear the brunt of her discontent. He'd have to find a way, somehow, to change things.

He made the weak tea and toast in silence and took it back to the bedroom. Thinking of this woman who was to bear his child caused a surge of love and warmth to well up in his heart. He'd protect Cleo from unnecessary pain, even if it was inflicted by his own mother!

As the days and weeks rolled by, Cleo moved into the next stage of her pregnancy, far more comfortable than the first. She began to round out nicely and felt wonderfully alive and serene. There was a doctor homesteading to the north, and her mother-in-law had told her rather tartly of several midwives in the area. But Tom had promised to move her to Pecos or Midland before the baby came, so she could go to the lying-in clinic.

In letters to her parents, Cleo wrote glowingly of her life on the ranch, discouraging them from making a trip to see her since she would be bringing their grandchild to

Houston as soon as possible after the baby was born. It was not that she didn't want to see them. The truth was that she was ashamed for her parents to know about her living conditions and the dreadful impasse with her mother-in-law.

In December, her father had a mild heart attack. That solved the problem of keeping her parents at bay, but his illness wasn't serious enough to merit a visit from Cleo. Life rocked along as she waited for the baby. And except for the constant subtle friction with her mother-in-law, she was happy.

A few weeks later, a brief warming trend brought an invitation to a social to be held on a ranch to the east of them. Cleo was more than ready for some entertainment to break the long monotony of her existence. Even Mrs. Kinney was excited. Dances were held on a more or less regular basis, depending on the weather, and everyone in the county was invited.

The ranch they approached was much like the one they had left many hours ago, with the mandatory windmill and tank. But the yard was filled with every type of conveyance and a large assortment of children of all ages. Though it was early evening, the sun hovered on the horizon, an orange pumpkin bobbing toward the stark black line of earth below.

The lively beat of country music, led by a whining violin, rolled out to greet them, and the sound of thumping feet invited them to join in. They were met at the door by their host and hostess, who shouted a welcome over the din.

C.J. "Crook" O'Tool was nicknamed for his back, not for his profession. As a young man he had been stomped by a horse, leaving him slightly stooped. Now he was in his late forties. His face was like a map of the country, reddish with white patches and sunspots, and there was a white line on his forehead where his hat never let the sun touch his skin.

Perched on his beaked nose were wire-rimmed glasses. It was a kindly face, filled with humor and goodwill.

"Howdy, y'all come right in." He stuck out a big rough paw to the men and nodded formally to the two women. "Y'all know my wife, Ina Mae, don't ya?"

Ina Mae ushered them toward a table filled to overflowing with venison, antelope, wild hog, rabbit and beef cooked in a dozen different recipes. There was a large complement of vegetables and desserts, too. "Hep yourselves, and be sure to save room for the real dessert, y'all hear? We've got iced tea for now and 'nilla ice cream for later. C.J. got three hunderd pounds of ice, so don't be bashful. The boys are out turnin' the dasher right now." She smiled up at Tom. "You shore got yourself a purty one, Tom. Guess she was worth waitin' for, huh?" She jabbed her sharp elbow into his ribs and laughed a big barrel laugh that filled her thin frame and shook her graying pompadour.

"Why, thank you, Mrs. O'Tool. She's a doozie, all right," Tom replied.

Cleo cringed a little, hearing the pure Texas drawl come out of her husband's mouth. She wasn't accustomed to it yet, though he seemed to be able to fit in with any audience. She smiled, accepting her hostess's compliment.

They ate heartily, and Cleo especially enjoyed the iced tea. There was even lemon to go in it. Though it was late winter, the promise of spring was in the air, and inside the crowded house, it was already as hot as the Fourth of July. She fanned her flushed face with one of Ina Mae's fancy napkins.

All the furniture in the big front room had been moved out, except for a line of chairs rimming the room. The men providing the music were playing a fiddle, a guitar, a harmonica and a big upright piano, and they performed with enthusiasm, if not skill.

Cleo spotted Leaf Kirby and her family. The owner of the general store and his wife smiled and waved, but outside of these few, she didn't recognize anyone. Much of the evening was spent in introductions to her "neighbors," the friendly folk who lived on the outlying ranches.

She and Tom danced together often. Especially the waltzes. Tom was an expert. "Gets it from his pa," Mrs. Kinney informed her.

As she sat out a dance to catch her breath, Cleo spotted Tom dancing with Leaf Kirby during one of the square dances. But he was soon spinning back to Cleo and swept her into his arms with such enthusiasm that all her doubts faded away.

Even the children danced with any willing partner. But as the hour grew later, the younger ones began to disappear. And when Cleo peeked into the adjoining rooms, she found some of the children already asleep on pallets spread out everywhere. They had eaten their ice cream and had gone to sleep with smiles on their faces. She closed the door softly and returned to her seat.

While Tom danced with his mother, Cleo became aware of the woman sitting beside her. The woman's face was strong-featured and a warm smile lighted her steel-gray eyes as she introduced herself. "I'm Tante Olga. Everyvun calls me that," she said in a heavy German accent. "Velcome to Vest Texas. I hope you vill be happy here. I see you are expecting a kinder. I am midvife, if you need me. I bring many kinder into the volrd."

"Wh—why, that's very kind of you, Tante Olga," Cleo said, not knowing quite how to reply. "I'm planning to go to Midland or Pecos when my time comes. But if I need you, it's nice to know you're there."

Tante Olga nodded sagely. "Sometimes first kinder aren't so eager to come into the vorld. Sometimes they come too early. You are strong and young, but doctors are far away. I am near. You send for me, and I vill come."

Cleo was mesmerized by the great strength and kindness she saw in the woman's eyes. Here was someone to lean on. She felt tiny shards of tears splinter in her own eyes. "Thank you, Tante Olga. I'll call you if I need you." Something in Olga reminded Cleo of her own mother, a faint chord of memory plucked softly. And then Tom was back to dance her around the floor and introduce her to yet another group of latecomers.

At first, the other men had been shy about asking Cleo to dance, until her host glided her around the room in a dignified waltz. "Crook" spun her away from him, still holding her hand, then brought her back to him. He covered a lot of ground with his long legs, showing her off with his twirls and spins, and then gallantly returned her to Tom with a slight bow. "Your little wife's a mighty fine dancer, young man. Yes sir, a mighty fine dancer."

Tom was about to agree when suddenly a shot rang out. The room fell instantly silent as several of the men sprinted for the door to see what had happened. But before they could investigate, a boy of around twelve staggered inside, holding a smoking pistol.

"I got 'im, Pa. I got 'im," he gasped, and collapsed on the floor.

His mother cradled her son's head in her lap, while his father ripped his shirt open. There, on the boy's neck, was a neat set of fang marks. The father patted his shoulder awkwardly as the mother rocked him, crooning pitifully.

"I'm so sorry, Hardy, I'm so sorry," said Crook, realizing that the child's life had already been snuffed out.

"Boy should have knowed better than to sleep on the ground this time of year," replied Hardy huskily, tears filling his eyes. "Snake probably crawled up into the blanket with him. At least it was quick, for I'd a hated to see him die by inches."

The couple was clearly stunned, barely able to take in the tragedy that had befallen them. Crook handed Hardy a mug of strong black coffee, and Ina Mae gave one to his wife.

"W—would you wantta bury him out here?" Crook asked hesitantly. "It would save the folks some travel time, and we can lay him out just as easy. We'd be honored to do it if you give the word." He paused. "Circuit rider ain't goin' to be around for a spell, so I'll read the service myself . . . iffen you're not up to it."

Mr. Hardy glanced over at his wife. With quiet tears streaming down her face, she nodded her consent. "Thank'ee kindly. I'm prayin' we'll never have to return the favor," she said in a strangled voice. She allowed the boy's body to be removed, and the Hardys were led into another room.

Cleo's face was ashen. "We'll spend the night here?" she whispered to Tom.

"Yes, we can sleep in the wagon. There's plenty of room and blankets."

Her skin prickled in horror. "But that boy was sleeping outside," she protested.

"He was sleeping on the ground," Tom reminded her. "We'll be up in the wagon, safe and sound. Snakes don't climb wagon wheels." When he saw the real terror in her eyes, he put his arms around her. "Don't worry. We'll be as safe as if we were in our bed at home."

But despite the warmth of her husband's embrace and his vow that he wouldn't leave her for a moment, Cleo slept little that night and was limp with exhaustion the next morning, when the sun appeared over the barren plain.

At breakfast, cooked over a campfire built by one of the men, there was time to get better acquainted with Ina Mae

O'Tool, who had brought out enough provisions to feed all who had stayed for the funeral.

"We come in nineteen and ten," Ina Mae said in answer to Cleo's question. "Set up housekeepin' in two half tents. They wuz floored and walled up for three feet." She lifted her head proudly. "I put down my best Brussels carpet. Figgered the sand might ruin it, but I wasn't gonna live like a savage even if I did have to live in the sand." Her gaze sobered. "'Course the sand did chew it up some. Guess you noticed the bare floor last night. Finally had to put that rug away. That near broke my heart. But I've learned to live with the land, not agin it. The time will come when I'll put down my fancy rug agin. Just as soon as we git rain and the market goes back up, we'll be sittin' purty. J.C. is a hard worker. We've never gone hungry." She grinned. "Sometimes it wasn't what we wanted to eat, but we always had somethin'. Some folks ain't so lucky. J.C. says the Smithtons are leavin'. Jest can't hang on no more. He's gonna try and find work in Midland. Land's for sale. Thank heavens we don't have no ready cash, or J.C. would buy it fer sure!"

"You don't want more land?" Cleo was puzzled.

"Honey, what'd we do with more land? Got thousands of acres right now. Got more land than sense. J.C. has it in his brain that he wants to own this half of Texas. Don't know why. It's jest all that much more work, if you ask me."

Cleo thought of what Tom had said about owning the land. Must be something men felt. She shrugged Tom's leather jacket closer around her.

Ina Mae smiled at Cleo. "Law me! I've done all the talkin'. When is that baby of yours due, and are you goin' to the laying-in sanitarium at Tante Olga's or are you goin' to Midland or Pecos to have that little cowboy?"

"Tom said he'd move me into town." Cleo dropped her

eyes. "It's my first one, so I'd like a regular doctor to deliver it." Quickly she added, "Nothing against Tante Olga, of course."

"'Course not. I 'spect I'd feel the same way if I'd had any choices. But if you do need her, she's the best in the whole state. She jest kinda naturally has this healin' touch . . . gift of God I'd call it. 'Course no one got a chance to do anything for the boy last night."

"Are there other children?" Cleo asked.

Ina Mae sighed. "All they have left are those three litte girls. They lost another boy a couple of years back. It'll be hard on him. He's gonna have to hire out all his work with no sons to help him. The girls may be able to help some, but it takes a man to do ranchin'. You'll find that out all too soon. Boys make the difference whether a man can make a go of a place or not."

Cleo considered what Ina Mae had told her as she rode with Tom over to the burial place. Tom had left his ranch, and now it was in bad shape. Was it his fault, or Robert's? Panic overtook her at the thought of Tom being tied to the land for years instead of only months.

During the short funeral service, where the mother sat trance like, there was more time to think. Though Cleo had never spent much time dwelling on God, outside of the mandatory Sunday school classes and church attendance with her family, she was beginning to believe that the only way to cope with this fearsome wilderness was to beseech the Almighty for His protection. *Dear Lord,* she prayed sincerely. *Comfort this family in their sorrow. And keep Tom and the baby and me safe.*

By the time they got home, Cleo was sleeping soundly against Tom's shoulder. She roused when the wagon pulled to a stop and, over her protests, he carried her into the house and tucked her into bed. "You rest for a while. A nap will do you good. Ma can take care of the cooking. Sleep, honey." She didn't argue, but snuggled into the feather pillows and nodded off again.

"Well, well," clucked Mrs. Kinney as Cleo entered the kitchen the next morning. "Finally finished your beauty nap, I see."

Cleo wanted nothing more than some good hot coffee to clear her head. She poured a cup and ignored the sarcastic remark, determined not to be goaded into an argument with her mother-in-law. "Good morning. Where's Tom?"

"Out where he's supposed to be. Robert, too. Workin' and gettin' things lined out for the roundup. Someone has to do the chores around here."

Cleo flushed at the implication. "What can I do to help?"

Mrs. Kinney eyed her blossoming figure. "Not much in your condition. 'Course, I was plowin' a truck garden when I was as far along as you, but you bein' so delicate, I don't think you should help me plant the potatoes."

"I can plant," Cleo insisted. "I'll be careful. Actually, I'm very strong and healthy. It's just that I want to do everything right for this baby," she said somewhat defensively.

Mrs. Kinney cleared her throat pointedly. "Heard you're trying to move off to Midland or Pecos to have that baby." She turned from her soapy dishwater. "Just where do you think we're goin' to get the money for you to live in town?" She shook her head. "We don't have no money to be wastin'." She looked accusingly at Cleo. "You think you're the first woman to ever have a baby out here? I had four. Yes, four. Two dead before they ever got to their first birthdays. But nowadays, women think they got to go live in Midland to have a baby. Pshaw!"

This was the first time Mrs. Kinney had leveled an open

attack on Cleo. She gasped under the force of the stinging rebuke. But now, words she had been storing in the reservoirs of her heart welled up, begging to be spoken. Cleo set her cup unsteadily on the table in front of her and took a deep breath.

"Mrs. Kinney, it wasn't my idea that Tom and I move out here. I hadn't planned to have a baby yet, either. And if I'd looked the world over, I'd never have chosen *you* for a mother-in-law. You've done nothing but bait me the entire time I've been here. You've even used silence to keep distance between us . . . you, who should know better than anyone what a treasure it is to have another woman to talk to in this lonely place!"

Cleo's rage was building. "Just know that I love your son with all my heart. And he chose me as his wife . . . for the rest of our lives! You'll just have to learn to accept that fact or . . ." here, she paused significantly, her voice softening ominously, "risk losing him."

"Well, you do have some spunk in you, after all." Mrs. Kinney was deadly calm, but her icy eyes shot sparks. "You're right about some of the things you said. But I'll never be satisfied that you're the one for my son until you prove to me that you can do somethin' for him besides sit around in fancy duds!"

"Give me some time, and I can make a *real* home for him," Cleo challenged. "I've got the money and the taste to do it."

Mrs. Kinney turned white. "This is my home, and I'll thank you to keep a civil tongue in your head."

"You don't want to be friends," Cleo continued with a wondering tone. "You want a contest for Tom's love." A sudden thought dawned on her. "And you weren't sick. At least not with anything a doctor could cure." Cleo's eyes narrowed as if seeing Mrs. Kinney for the first time. "You couldn't stand the thought of Tom and me living the good life in Houston while you and Robert scratched out a living in the sand. You were *jealous,*" she breathed. "All this time I thought *I* needed to do something to win your approval. But it's *you. You* have the problem."

Mrs. Kinney had slumped against the cabinet, clutching a wet tea towel against her chest. "How dare you speak to me like that!" she hissed. "And in my own home. Get out, and take all your things with you! Get out!"

Cleo eyed her coolly. "And if I do, who do you think will follow me? Who will leave you with only Robert to help with the ranch?" Steady hands picked up the cup and re-filled it. "You'd better think twice before issuing an ulti-matum like that. I can shut down this little family business just by walking out that door."

Mrs. Kinney straightened and drew a deep breath. "Yes, I suppose you could. You're a cold, heartless woman, Cleo . . . Kinney . . . but I'm glad to see that Tom didn't marry a spineless little rabbit. He'll need a strong wife out here." There was a flicker of admiration in the pale eyes.

The two women had made no peace pact nor negotiated any terms. But Cleo knew she had won something this day. With a heady rush of power, she watched the woman go outside to feed her chickens. Never in her life had she spo-ken to anyone the way she had just now. The sensation of euphoria quickly subsided, replaced by panic as she won-dered if Mrs. Kinney would say anything to Tom and just as quickly decided she probably would not wish to betray her own defeat. She knew the rivalry was not over. Nor the silences. Only the snide little remarks and catty digs.

As the day wore on, Cleo continued to feel a niggling doubt about the wisdom of her outburst. Up until now she had buried her own feelings of hostility toward her mother-in-law. Then something had snapped and she had said things that should have been left unsaid. She couldn't really be sure Mrs. Kinney wouldn't tell Tom. What if he sided with his mother?

In desperation, Cleo prayed, *Lord, please get me out of this mess!* Then she felt a flush of defiance. *But I won't apologize. What I said was true. Just please don't let her tell Tom, and I'll promise never to lose my temper with her again.* At least, she would try not to.

She and Tom had to get away from here. They needed a house of their own, or even one room. She would have to speak to Tom about it tonight.

"Honey, you know there's no money to build a house," Tom said with a sigh of defeat. He was propped on his elbow in bed, leaning over to stroke Cleo's small rounded belly through the quilt.

She looked up sorrowfully. "You know what's going on in this house between your mother and me, don't you?" She tried to read the truth in his eyes. Did he know about the fight she'd had with his mother this morning? She didn't think so.

He lay back on the pillows, hands behind his head. "Yes, I know. Maybe if I speak to her. . . ."

"No," she said quickly, "there's no need to talk to her. Just do something. Your mother loves you, Tom, and she doesn't want to share you. Think about it. She's all alone. But if we don't get some distance between us soon, one of us is in big trouble." The warning tone in her voice left no doubt about that.

"You can complain until the cows come home, but there's no money to build another house." A slow grin crossed his face. "Let's find her a husband, instead."

Cleo sat up straight. "What?!"

"I meant it as a joke."

"But . . . maybe it's a good idea," she mused. "She'd have somebody else to help with the ranch besides you and Robert."

Tom shrugged. "Well, I'm not so sure I'd want any of the bachelors around here to marry my mama. That could lead to problems of another kind. But," he began, his eyes brightening, "maybe we could build on a little section to the back of the house. We could share the kitchen. I could dog trot it so there'd be a little space between the house and the room," he said thoughfully.

"Oh, that would be wonderful! I could fix it up and make a place for the three of us . . . a real retreat. Oh, Tom, how soon can we start?"

"You know the roundup has to come first right now. It'll take two or three weeks to get the cattle gathered and branded. Then I'll have to drive some of them to Monahans for shipping." He kissed her sweetly. "But we'll get around to the building as soon as possible," he promised. "I'm sure I can get some of the men to work with me after roundup. Ranchers are used to helping each other out."

Cleo wasn't especially thrilled to hear Tom speak of himself as part of the brotherhood of ranchers, but she knew he'd keep his promise. That room would ease the strain of living in this wilderness with a woman who seemed to hate her.

She snuffed out the light, gave a deep sigh, and snuggled into the pillows. *But how long, Lord, how long?* She looked toward the heavens, but she didn't expect an answer.

# seven

Though every tortured muscle in his body was complaining, Tom was exhilarated from his physical labor. The roundup was going well. He and his fellow ranchers had driven the scattered cattle into a a pasture for holding, and he was pleased with the number of calves that had been added to his herd. Still, there was always the worry about having to buy more fodder to feed them, he fretted silently. A rancher's curse. He wanted more—more cattle, more land. But times were hard, and he couldn't afford to buy any more, so he was determined not to let one acre slip through his fingers. More and more people were moving into the area, and more and more land was being bought up, land he wanted. *If I can just hold on until the drought breaks,* he thought, *I can expand.*

Ever since returning to the ranch, the obsession to acquire more land had gripped him. He was sure that in time, especially now that he had promised Cleo a little place of her own, he would be able to convince her to stay. He was deeply contented working the land again, with his wife at his side and a baby on the way. It would be a fitting legacy to pass on to the next generation of Kinneys.

The only rock in his bed was the relationship between Cleo and his mother. Tom had looked on from the beginning, and knew things were not easy for Cleo. His mother hadn't cut her any slack, but at least there were fewer barbed remarks, and he took this as a good sign.

The smell of scorching hair and flesh assailed his senses, and Tom reined in his wandering thoughts to address the task at hand. He had a good horse, a cow pony who knew how to work the cattle, thus saving the rider a lot of work. Today he was cutting out calves for branding, castrating, and earmarking. Yesterday he had worked on the ground, and his back was sore from the strenuous bending and stretching. It felt good to lean back in the saddle while the horse pulled the rope tight.

They broke for lunch, and wearily he accepted the inevitable beans and sowbelly and a mug of hot coffee that singed the hair off his tongue.

"Don't you have any iced tea?" he complained to the cook.

A wave of laughter broke out among the cowboys sitting under the mesquite trees. "Go soak your head in the stock tank iffen you want to cool off, Tom," advised Crook.

Tom sank down in the scant shade next to Crook and Robert, and the three of them ate in silence for a few moments, each lost in his own world. Conversation was never a prerequisite for friendship on the range, and each man respected the others' right to contemplation.

It was Crook who shattered the silence when he spoke up, pointing with his knife at a figure riding into camp. "Well, look who's here, Tom! The little lady!"

Tom jumped up to help Cleo down off the mare. "What are you doing out here?" The displeasure in his voice was undisguised.

Cleo, not expecting a reprimand, pouted prettily. "Why, I wanted to see what a roundup was all about, darling. I need to know about your work, Tom." She walked under a mesquite, pulling off her hat and fanning herself.

"Women don't belong out here. It's too dangerous," he said flatly. "Not only that, you shouldn't be bouncing around on a horse right now."

She gave Tom a withering look. "I'm a very good rider. Besides, I walked the mare part of the way."

"And if she'd gotten spooked, you might have lost the baby."

"She didn't, and I didn't." Cleo tried a dazzling smile to charm him out of his foul mood. "Could I have a little something to eat? I'm famished."

Reluctantly he brought her a plate of food and a cup of coffee. "Sit here and don't get in anybody's way. We've got work to do."

Cleo couldn't swallow over the large lump of anger and tears knotted in her throat, but she sipped at her coffee, hoping the scalding brew would help. With the branding fire only a short distance from where she sat, she found herself with a front-row seat to a calf-roping. Or was it? The men were so deft with the knife that at first she couldn't be sure what they were doing. A swift slice, the sudden bawl of the calf, and then she knew. For one awful moment she thought she was going to gag. Quickly she got to her feet, putting the chuck wagon between herself and the activity around the fire.

Just at that moment an enormous man came from around the tailgate. "Would you like something to settle your stomach, Missus?" he asked kindly.

Though not much taller than she, the man had to weigh close to three hundred pounds, she thought. He was wearing a clean white starched shirt and a big apron over his clothes. With garters on his sleeves to hold up the cuffs, he looked more like a bartender or a gambler than a cowboy.

"Yes, thank you." Gratefully she accepted the cup he offered her.

"Peppermint tea. Best thing for an upset stomach. Always keep some handy. Use it myself sometimes when the smell out here gets to me," he said apologetically. He tipped his hat to her. "Smallwood's the name, though everone here'bouts calls me Fatty."

"The tea does help, uh . . . Mr. Smallwood." She couldn't bring herself to call him by the nickname. "Is your ranch around here?"

"Oh, no, ma'am. No self-respectin' horse'd let me on his back. I have a café in Midland, and I run a chuck wagon for the ranchers at spring roundup time. But my daddy used to go on the long trail drives. This here's his very own wagon." He lovingly caressed the wood on the wagon bed.

"I've never seen a real chuck wagon."

"Then come around back, ma'am. Here's the best part." He showed her how the tailgate acted as a small two-legged table and how a cabinet had been built in the back of the wagon with drawers and compartments to hold the staples and cooking gear. It was quite ingenious and compact. "Cook also acts as a doc, especially on a drive. I enjoy comin' out here in the spring, but I'd never survive a real drive. 'Course, ain't many of those no more. Fartherest I've ever been was to Pecos and Monahans." He pulled his hat down more firmly on his big ears. "Yes, sir, times have changed."

Cleo glanced in the direction of her working husband. Apparently Tom had no intention of spending any more time with her. Besides, she was furious at him for treating her with such indifference.

As if reading her thoughts, Fatty cleared his throat. "Ah, ma'am, I wuz plannin' on goin' back in, since I don't feed the men their supper. If you'd care to ride along with me, I'll swing by your place." He all but stubbed his toe in the dirt in his embarrassment at being so bold as to ask to accompany her home.

Cleo favored him with a bright smile. "Why, that would be lovely, Mr. Smallwood." She started for the wagon.

"Ma'am, you'd do better ridin' that sweet mare. This here seat bounces like an unbroke bronc. But you stick close by the wagon. Snakes is bad this time of year, and I noticed you ain't carryin' no gun."

She looked around with concern. "I didn't see any on the ride out, though my horse did shy a few times. Do you suppose . . ." She left the sentence unfinished, but felt the finger of fear prod her spine at the thought.

Riding home, Cleo gradually relaxed. Fatty had keen eyesight and a ready rifle and fired at regular intervals . . . "jest to make sure."

As he told her, "Rattlers is the curse of the land, not the sand."

"Don't the cattle ever get bitten?" she inquired.

"Oh, sometimes, but you put a snake in a herd of cattle, and he's most likely to get hisself stomped to death before he can make up his mind who to bite first."

Cleo laughed out loud. "Have *you* ever been bitten?"

"Well, no ma'am. Guess they figger I'm too big, but I wuz almost *licked* to death by one onct," he replied with a wide grin.

She laughed again as she envisioned that scene.

"It's a real pleasure to see a fine-lookin' woman enjoyin' herself," Fatty observed. "That Tom is as lucky as a dog with two tongues."

Cleo could not hide another smile. "Are you married, Mr. Smallwood?" she asked with interest.

Fatty positively blushed. "Why, no, ma'am. No gal would ever take me serious, I reckon. Had an endurin' friendship with a lady of the evenin' until she moved to the big city, though. Right purty thing, she was. You put me in mind of her, your black hair and all." Quickly he added, "No offense intended. It's just that I've always been a fancier of beautiful women. Like to watch 'em, and all their dainty ways."

"Why, I'm not offended. I'm flattered." She looked at

him from under the brim of her hat. "I've seldom met a man as honest and forthright as you, Mr. Smallwood. I hope we'll be friends."

"My ma always said there wasn't nothin' between my brain and my mouth, so the words just ran out." He laughed. "It's got me in a heap o' trouble a few times."

"I understand how easy that can be," she confessed, "getting oneself in trouble, I mean." Then she told him about the bathing beauty escapade.

They shared the telling of the tale with mutual good humor, and then Fatty said, "I can see how come you'd think it was all right to be out here on the roundup, then. Tom didn't know he'd got hisself a live one, I reckon. You'll be good for him, I expect. He's a careful man, Tom is. He could use a little livenin' up. And his mama is a good woman and a hard worker, but she's about as much fun as eatin' chile with a burnt tongue."

Cleo laughed her agreement. "Humor is not her strong suit. But I think we're coming to an understanding." For the remainder of the trip, Cleo found herself telling Fatty all sorts of private things, things she had never dreamed she would confide to anyone but Mattie. He was a sympathetic listener. And he didn't offer advice. He merely listened, nodding and grinning on occasion. She was disappointed when she saw the ranch house come into view, for the ride was almost over, and there would be only the dour Mrs. Kinney waiting for her there.

Cleo moved her horse closer to the wagon and put out her hand. "Thank you for seeing me home, Mr. Smallwood. I truly had a wonderful time and hope we'll meet again soon."

"Just one more thing, ma'am. Would you call me Fatty? It would make me mighty happy."

She smiled. "Only if you call me Cleo." And they sealed their new friendship with a handshake.

Fatty was clattering off as Cleo opened the door to the house. Needing a cool drink of water from the gravity flow tap, she went into the kitchen where she found Mrs. Kinney cutting up one of her non-laying hens for supper.

"Could have told you not to go. Tom was mad, wasn't he?" her mother-in-law muttered. And not waiting for an answer, she hurried on. "Women don't belong at a roundup." Softly she added, "Everyone knows that." There was no mistaking the satisfaction behind the words.

Cleo's chin lifted defiantly. "Yes, he was mad, but I'm still glad I went. First, I now feel that I understand my husband's work a little better. And secondly, I got to meet Mr. Smallwood. I was very impressed."

Mrs. Kinney shrugged. "Doesn't take much to impress you, I guess. Fatty is just . . . Fatty."

For one crazy moment Cleo wondered if they could marry her mother-in-law off to the man. Maybe some of his kindness would rub off and melt the crust of bitterness Tom's mother had built up around herself. Cleo giggled a little at the notion. And when Mrs. Kinney turned to stare, she explained inanely, "He made me laugh."

Unaccountably, the woman looked off at the rolling prairie framed by the kitchen window and began to share. "Fatty came to call once when I was a young girl livin' in Midland. He was as irresponsible then as he is now. Playin' cowboy the way he does. Why, by now he should have built that little café into a fine big restaurant."

Cleo darted a sidelong glance at her mother-in-law. "Maybe he would have . . . if he'd had a good wife to help him."

"Humph," she grunted. "Man's a dreamer, not a doer. He'd of never made it out here on a ranch. Good thing he stayed in town."

Cleo gave up. She wasn't about to change Mrs. Kinney's

mind so easily, and she deplored hearing Fatty ridiculed. So she went to her room to get out of her riding togs and into something more comfortable. Looking up, she was surprised to see her mother-in-law standing in the doorway.

"Changin' clothes again? I declare, I never knew anyone who wore as many duds in a week as you do, but then I never had that many myself," Mrs. Kinney commented, her lips thinned in disapproval. "Just came by to tell ya one of the men left some buildin' lumber out back. What's it for?"

Cleo finished buttoning her blouse and turned to look the woman directly in the eye. "It's for the new room Tom's adding on for the two of us and the baby." She waited, but there was no reply, only a crumpling of the blanched face. The woman left without a word, and Cleo smiled a tiny smile of triumph.

The smile faded when she heard Tom's booted tread on the porch. She hurried to meet him, eager to make things right between them. Despite his dust-covered clothing and the stench of the corral, she hugged him close and mumbled her apology into the warmth of his shoulder.

He patted her awkwardly. "It's all right, honey. I was just surprised to see you, and I was tired and hot. But," he warned, "I don't want you out there again . . . not until after the baby is born."

She breathed a sigh of relief over this swift absolution and gave him her promise. And later before she slept, she thanked God for Tom's love. *Please don't ever let him stop loving me,* she prayed, vaguely aware that prayer was becoming a vital part of her everyday life.

Cleo was gradually becoming accustomed to the inconveniences of living on a ranch. Though she did not relish the chores, keeping busy with the cooking, cleaning, and washing did help to prevent those painful confrontations with her mother-in-law. And she enjoyed the outdoor gardening tasks. Still, fresh vegetables in turn required canning and storing, and Cleo hated canning days.

The kitchen was like an inferno, and she felt faint and limp when it was over. She did nothing she thought would hurt the baby, but she took grim satisfaction in being able to keep up with Mrs. Kinney. No one could say she wasn't doing her share of the work.

Her one real joy was caring for her rosebushes. When Mrs. Smithington left, she had given the bushes to Ina Mae, who in turn had passed them on to Cleo, with lots of advice on how to raise them. Cleo had listened carefully, then had planted them in a sheltered area under the bedroom window, where she would be able to enjoy them all summer long. No matter how tired she was, she tended them daily. They were budding now, with the promise of heavenly blooms very soon.

True to his word, To had enlisted the aid of some of the ranchers and they had come to help him frame up the new room. It was about half-finished now, and Cleo was wild with the desire to go to town to purchase the things they'd need.

Knowing how scarce money was, Tom had tried to hold her down. Being a fair carpenter, he could trade for the wood and build some of the furnishings himself. But she was dead set on recreating a room she'd seen in one of those ladies' magazines, and she wouldn't be satisfied with home-made furniture or hand-me-downs. And she wanted one of those fancy baby beds—a cast iron one, painted white, all fluff and frills.

When Tom had been less than enthusiastic, Cleo had pouted. Men didn't understand such things, she fumed inwardly. They were so doggedly practical! Anyway, she'd planned to use her own money to furnish the room. Though she had left the bulk of her dowry in the bank in Houston, she had a hundred dollars secreted in her big traveling trunk. Tom wouldn't want her to use it. But since it hadn't been enough to save the ranch—and after his last impassioned speech about his manly need to fix things by himself, she wouldn't have risked damaging his ego by offering it—she'd kept quiet about it.

Now she had a use for that money, one she could justify, since it would be used for Tom and the baby as well as for herself. And mentally planning how she would decorate their room had kept her sane in all the long hours she'd spent under Mrs. Kinney's roof.

Cleo was working with her roses when she noticed that the day was growing sultry, an oddity in this dry country. While the sun was baking the earth as it did every day, something did not feel quite right, and she remarked about it to Mrs. Kinney.

"Storm's probably on the way. I noticed thunderheads buildin'."

When Cleo scanned the horizon, she could see only a tiny cloud that appeared no larger than her hand. "You mean it might rain?"

"Maybe. Might just storm. We've had dry storms before."

The preoccupation with the weather that was peculiar to West Texas annoyed Cleo. In Houston, a cloudy day usually signaled rain with occasional rolling thunder. But, hurricane weather excepted, it was an uneventful thing.

Here, every cloud was examined and commented on, every sign observed and attached to the story of some former storm, or lack of. The wind was constantly monitored, and any change noted. Since the wind blew every day from some direction, it was an unflagging topic of conversation.

Cleo had endured Texas bragging all her life, but never

had she lived where it was hotter, drier, or windier. It remained to be seen if it could be wetter, too. And seeing that the clouds had spread along the horizon in a thin black line, she decided that they might be about to get some rain, after all.

At that moment Tom came wheeling in on his horse. "Get everything battened down! Get the chickens in the barn! Everything, inside!"

"But, Tom, the clouds are so far away," she protested.

"Honey, those aren't rain clouds. That's a black duster, and it's headed this way as sure as sunrise. Now get going! I'll put the horses in the barn."

The look on his face frightened her. "Sand? Is that all?"

"Sometimes behind the sand is a big storm. I don't like the looks of this one. We're likely to have cattle in the next state before it's all over. Now go, and then get into the house. Quick!"

It was as if a giant blanket was being pulled slowly over them from the ground. Cleo watched from the porch as the boiling black sand moved inexorably toward them. And with the approach of the storm came a gentle twilight as the sand blocked out the sun.

She leaned closer to Tom when he joined her, shucking off his sweat-stained hat. "It really is a black sandstorm, isn't it? It's getting as dark as night."

He nodded, frowning. "Seems like we can't have a few clouds gather and drop a little rain on us. To get rain we have to have a major storm, and then we may not get anything at all but mud falling out of the sky."

Cleo was puzzled. "Mud?"

"Just enough rain to wet down the sand. When it falls, it's mud."

She sighed. "I shouldn't be surprised, I suppose. Apparently anything can happen in this part of Texas. Now I believe some of the tales I've been hearing." She moved closer to Tom as the darkness deepened and the edges of the storm approached. He took her inside and shut the door, dropping a big piece of wood into metal slots on each side of the door frame.

Robert and his mother came in from the barn, and the four of them gathered in the kitchen, by common agreement the safest place. Shutters had been closed over the few windows of the house, and they begin to jiggle and bang in their confinement as the wind picked up.

Mrs. Kinney lit the lamp, and they sat around the table, listening. The wind howled, hurling sand against the house with giant fingers. At first, the grains made a pinging sound, but it was soon swalllowed up in the fierceness of the storm. It was awesome to be trapped inside the house in the eerie darkness.

"Tom," Robert said softly. "Do you hear it?"

Tom's face looked suddenly drawn and haggard. "I hear it. Under the table, everyone."

Everyone except Cleo sprang into action. Robert sprinted to the bedrooms, dragged blankets off the beds, and brought them back. Mrs. Kinney blew out the lamp. Tom covered Cleo with a blanket.

"What is it, Tom?" Cleo was pale with fright.

"A cyclone, most likely. With any luck, though, it'll miss us."

"Sounds like the train coming into Monahans," Robert observed.

The wind changed from a howl to a shriek, rattling the windows and shaking the very foundations of the house. This was followed by a soft plunking sound that gained in intensity. Faster and faster.

"Hail," said Mrs. Kinney. "We're in for it now. It always hails before a cyclone." She closed her eyes in prayer and her lips moved as she begged the Almighty for His mercy.

In her fright Cleo prayed, too, a childish litany of entreaty. *Dear Lord Jesus, don't let it hit us, please! Keep us safe. Please, Lord, don't let it hit us. Keep us safe. Help us, Lord. Please, dear God, don't let us die.*

Robert was praying out loud, and Tom mumbled under his breath.

The roar grew louder and the entire house quaked as if aware of what was coming. The groaning of boards and hinges was almost human, and then the monster wind began chewing its way over them, snapping and tearing in a frenzy of destruction.

For one awful moment Cleo thought she might faint, so terrifying was the sound. She could feel Tom's arms around her, holding her tightly, and she was aware of her heart beating beneath the scratchy woolen blanket he had pulled over her. The table danced a macabre dance over their heads. And then it was as still as death.

Cleo wondered if the storm had left her deaf until she heard Tom let out his breath. "It's over."

He crawled out from under the table and walked to the door. Cleo wanted to beg him not to open the door. The monster that had raged outside might still be out there. But he raised the heavy board and pushed away the sand that had piled up against the door. The sky beyond was cloudless and impossibly blue.

Cleo scrambled out, nearly losing her footing on the thin layer of grit that covered the kitchen floor. When she straightened her rumpled clothing and licked her dry lips, she felt as if she had been dipped in water and then carefully rolled across the beach. Everything she touched on her way to the back door was coated with sand.

"No rain," Tom said.

"No room," said Robert with rare dry wit as he looked

around to the side of the house.

Sure enough, all the careful building of the past few weeks was completely gone. Not a trace of it remained. Cleo was too shocked to cry. She could only stare stupidly.

"Barn roof is gone, too," Mrs. Kinney clucked her tongue sadly. "Wonder if the animals are all right? Oh, there's the tin roof . . . over there in the pasture." Obediently, they looked in the direction of her pointed finger. "But where is the chicken coop?"

It was found some hundred yards away, perched atop a mesquite tree, all the chickens safe inside, but without a feather left on any of their frightened bodies.

Mrs. Kinney laughed in relief. "Poor things look pitiful, don't they? But at least they're alive."

Robert came back with a report on the barn animals. "They're okay. Ranger kicked down most of his stall, but he ain't hurt."

Further inspection of the property revealed that the blades of the windmill next to the house were gone, too. It was easy to follow the path of the twister, where the tail had dipped down into the pasture and taken mesquite and grass with it. "Made us a road," said Robert.

"Yeah." Tom gave a short laugh. "But to where?"

Robert scratched his head. "Wherever you want it to lead to, I reckon."

"You saddle up and check on the cattle close around," Tom told his brother. "I'll go out to the far east pasture and check there. We may be having a big barbecue soon. And while I'm at it, I'll see if if anyone else had any damage. After I see to our stock, I'll ride over to the O'Tools."

Cleo was turning to go into the house when she remembered her roses. With a heavy heart she walked around to the sheltered side of the house. To her surprise, she found that while the canes looked a bit beaten up, the roses were still intact. She laughed out loud with relief. "Thank you, Lord, for keeping us safe from the storm! Thank you, thank you, thank you," she whispered into the blue sky as she fingered the buds tenderly.

Just beyond the roses, she saw a piece of hail the size of an apple. How odd to see ice lying on the sunbaked earth. But in this heat, it would be quickly gone. The chilled air was warming and things would soon be back to normal.

It had all happened so fast that it seemed like a dream. A very bad dream. But they were all safe. She and Tom and the baby. Robert. Even her mother-in-law. Cleo took one last look at the roses and hurried inside.

# eight

There was very little damage to any of the other spreads, so the ranchers and their wives turned out to make a day of reroofing the Kinneys' barn and putting up the frame for the additional bedroom. One of the cows that had broken its neck during the storm was barbecued, and the front room was cleared for dancing. It turned out to be a very festive occasion, and Cleo enjoyed it immensely, realizing again how fragile life is and how valuable one's friends. Robert, Tom, and Crook continued to work on the room for the next week, adding a little breezeway between the two structures, where they hung a porch swing for Cleo to enjoy the evening coolness.

It had taken tears, arguments, and compromise, but she had finally talked Tom into letting her use a little of the money she had put away to furnish the new room. She was thrilled that she would soon have a place to call her own.

From the Sears and Roebuck catalog, she ordered an ornate brass bed for them and the fancy baby crib she had wanted. With freight, the amount came to twenty-five dollars. She also ordered some floral printed fabric for curtains and a bedspread. Of course, Mrs. Kinney was scandalized at the "waste of money," but she made very few ripples in their pool of happiness.

When the room was finished, and the beds from Sears had been dragged through the sucking sand to the ranch, Cleo stood in the doorway and drank it all in. Soft lamplight glowed from the table beside the bed. The brass headboard shone, and the colorful bedspread looked inviting. The

Smithingtons' big chifforobe, contracted for by Tom when they moved out, stood to one side, and the baby bed waited serenely on the other wall. She smiled softly. It was worth everything she had endured.

"Someday I'll have a real home for you to live in," she said to her child. "Maybe not like the one I grew up in, but much nicer and bigger than this." She patted her stomach. "You come from good stock. Your grandparents in Houston are quite well-to-do. And someday your father will have this ranch on its feet. You wait and see." Tears gathered in her eyes. "But you'll never go hungry or ragged, I promise you. You'll always have the best I can give you."

The summer days were like the forged links in an overheated chain, too hot to touch, and they sizzled to an end, one by one.

In June, the garden was at its height, and canning went on all day. Cleo was sure she had sweated every ounce of fluid from her body by lunchtime each day. The men slaughtered a cow, and the thin strips of meat were hung over the barbed-wire fence to dry in the merciless sun. The meat could then be boiled or fried for a tasty dish in the winter.

Cleo stood beneath the lone tree in the front yard and gazed out over the trackless land. Heat waves shimmered above the ground and a steady, drying wind sucked the sweat from her clothes. The sky was a turquoise blue without a suggestion of a cloud. The prickly grass rustled in the slight breeze, and she could hear the cattle lowing distantly. At her feet was Old Jack, the mixed breed dog, panting and heaving in the heat. In the house she could hear the clinking of hot glass jars as they were released from their boiling bath, imagining the blistering steam rising from the vessel.

Cleo had let her hair grow out, and she lifted its heavy weight from the nape of her neck to catch whatever breeze was about. Well into her pregnancy, she felt the baby kick hard. "What are *you* complaining about," she asked grumpily. "You're perfectly comfortable. You should feel it out here." As if to make a point, the baby kicked her again.

Cleo closed her eyes and tried to will herself back to that day on the beach when she had first seen Tom. She tried to recreate the damp, salty sea breeze and the sound of the waves teasing the shore rhythmically. It was a hazy imagining and with it came a distinctly painful ache. She opened her eyes. "From sand and salt water to more sand and scarce water." She shrugged her shoulders helplessly. What was, was. She had a husband and a baby on the way. She had her own little retreat. It wasn't much, but it was everything.

She purposefully blocked the thought of her lovely Houston home and the friends there. She simply couldn't deal with that right now. She could only live in the present, one day at a time, for whenever she allowed herself to dwell on the fact that she might be stuck here for years, she was overwhelmed with hopelessness.

It had been more than nine months since she had seen her parents. Mail service from town was sporadic at best, for though it normally came in every two weeks, someone had to ride in to get it, and lately they hadn't been able to spare the time. But a trip to the post office always rewarded Cleo with letters from her mother. She would sit on the bed and arrange them by dates, savoring each one, carefully splitting the tops of the envelopes with a small pen knife, and then putting them in order in a little box. In between times she would reread them.

Her mother's letters, filled with news of home—social events, her father's health, and assurances of her love—always gave Cleo a lift. Sometimes she cried as she read, overcome by such love for her parents that it spilled from her eyes. And then the homesickness would threaten to drown her, until she thought of Tom and the baby. It was as if she were caught between two worlds—one in Houston with her parents and one here on the ranch with Tom.

Cleo tried to keep her own letters light, hoping the sadness didn't creep in between the lines. "I'm hoping to bring the baby to you at Christmas," she wrote. "Tomorrow we're going on a picnic. My first visit to the famous Sand Hills. A picnic in the sand sounds a lot like home, doesn't it?"

With the anticipated outing, it was a little easier to get to sleep, thinking of the welcome break in their dull routine.

"Hand me up that big basket, and mind you be careful, it's full of pies," ordered Mrs. Kinney as she stood in the back of the wagon. Cleo was carrying out old quilts for them to sit on in the dunes, while Robert and Tom dutifully loaded the mountain of food that had been prepared.

There had been a short discussion about the propriety of Cleo's appearing in public so late in her pregnancy. A very short discussion.

"If you think I'm ashamed of my condition, you're flat-dab crazy!" she said loudly enough for Mrs. Kinney to hear. "And I'm not going to miss the biggest party of the year because I stick out in front. That lump is *your child*, and I'm not ashamed of it. And you shouldn't . . ."

"Wait, wait, I give," Tom said laughingly, holding up his hands in mock surrender. "You win. I just thought, well, never mind what I thought." He kissed her tenderly, and she wore a loose-fitting smock that looked quite attractive on her. He was careful to tell her how pretty she looked.

The sun had barely rubbed the sleep out of its eyes when they were underway to the Sand Hills to celebrate the Fourth of July. But it seemed like more than half a day's travel before they reached the dunes and found the other revelers.

A huge tarp had been secured as a shelter underneath the

trees at the largest water hole toward the back of the dunes. Sawhorses had been set up and planks laid to make a table that was already groaning with food.

The sand was so bright from the blistering sun that Cleo had to squint to see where she was going as she helped carry their food to the makeshift table. It was awkward walking in the deep shifting sand, and her balance was impaired by both her pregnancy and the big basket of fried chicken she carried.

"Here, let me help you with that."

Still squinting, Cleo saw only a set of dazzling white teeth and then dark blue eyes, crinkling with good humor and sunlight, laughing out from under the brim of the Stetson.

She surrendered the basket to her rescuer. "Oh, thank you."

"I'm Delmore Albert Lennon, but everyone calls me Dal." He took her elbow to steady her in the sand as they walked. "I know who *you* are. You're the talk of the county." He flashed that smile again, his long legs propelling them quickly to the table, where he helped himself to one of the crispy pieces of chicken he had set down. "The spoils of battle," he declared as he bit deeply into a leg.

"Do you live on a ranch around here?"

"Yes, we have the spread west of yours, but your fame and beauty have spread even to the ends of the earth, otherwise known as the Rocking L Ranch."

"You look like a rancher," she said surveying his jeans and the bandana tucked into his shirt, "but you sure don't talk like one."    "Much to my papa's dismay, I've left the ranch behind me for now."   The confident smile appeared once more. "I'm an oil promoter. I've been working down in Ft. Stockton, but I've moved up here for now." His eyes scanned the horizon. "Someday this is going to be a rich oil country, in spite of what some folks say. There's oil under these big old pastures. I've been buying, selling, and holding some of the leases."

Cleo frowned. "You speculate, then."

"Yes, ma'am. Me and my partner have made some good money, too. We lease some land, dig a well, and pay the rancher, and everyone else who put something in the pot."

"You make it sound so simple," she said, intrigued in spite of herself.

"Well, it is, when the oil comes in. The only problem is when it doesn't." The tall stranger laughed.

Looking up, Cleo saw Tom walking toward them with a scowl on his face. "Do you know my husband Tom?" she asked when he had reached them.

"From when we was pups. How are you, Tom? Been getting to know your wife, here. Hope to be so lucky myself someday." His gaze was frankly admiring.

"You still selling those leases?" The way Tom pronounced the word, he might have been saying *rattlers*.

"Yep, wheeling and dealing all the time. You'd do well to consider leasing me some of your land." The man's eyes were as steady as a poker player calling a bluff.

Tom bristled. "Even if there was oil under my land, that's where I want it to stay. I'm a rancher."

"I won't give up on you, but I'll let you be . . . for now." Dal slapped him on the back. "Let's just celebrate the holiday." He tipped his hat to Cleo and wandered off to greet another group of men.

"Stay away from that snake-oil salesman," Tom said softly as he watched Dal make his pitch.

*The very idea!* Cleo fumed to herself. Why should Tom forbid her to talk to this charming man? But she sensed his jealousy and didn't argue.

It was an enjoyable day, an opportunity to spend time with her new friends. Tante Olga studied Cleo's ripening figure.

"You carry your baby high." She smiled. "A nice, fat little girl for you." Noting the sudden frown on Cleo's face, she was immediately solicitous. "You feel all right? You look tired."

"It's all the canning we've been doing in the heat, Tante Olga. I need a little rest, that's all."

Olga nodded in agreement. "I have a tonic that vill help you get your strength. You need to be strong for your delivery."

Cleo had a lot of questions to ask Olga, things she normally would have asked her own mother but would never have considered sharing with Mrs. Kinney. And as Olga answered, Cleo found herself growing impatient for the miracle to occur.

"Who could not believe in Gott when they see a newborn kinder? From the love of a man and woman comes a new life." Olga's face was soft with love. "And it is up to you and that man to love that little one and care for her. To teach her about Gott's love for her."

Cleo flushed, thinking of her own fragile faith. "I'm afraid I only call on Him when I'm in trouble," she confessed.

"It's a beginning. Now you can start to practice thanking Him, too. When it comes to raising kinder, I don't know vhat vomen who don't pray do. Ve can't control life around us. All ve can do is ask the Lord's mercy."

Cleo thought of the boy who had been bitten by the rattlesnake. Had his mother failed to pray for his safety?

"Read the Scriptures every day for the strength and courage to be happy in this hard land." Olga patted Cleo's hand. "And pray."

On impulse, Cleo seized her hand. "I want you to be there when the baby comes."

"I vill be there," Olga promised. Looking up, she shaded her eyes. "There is Miss Lemmon and her nephew. I think someone say he fall off his horse."

"Then you're needed. I'll talk with you later." Cleo's eyes glistened. "Thank you, Tante Olga."

Olga nodded and turned her attention to the boy.

Cleo helped herself to some iced tea, then found a seat under the shade of the big willows. It was a relief to be off her feet. The great, restless dunes around her radiated heat, and she was certain an egg could be cooked on the surface quickly.

Tom came and sat beside her on the blanket to polish off a big slab of chocolate cake.

"I can't believe there's water right here in the middle of all this sand," Cleo observed, seeing the great still pool, reeds lacing its face and willows swaying around the perimeter. "And those willows. They aren't like the weeping willows at home, but they're so large."

"Been used for years by Indians and people moving west," Tom said. "And over there is where a man claimed he found some mastadon bones. You can still see where the Indians made camp. See those smoky stones over there in a circle? A cooking fire."

Cleo's gaze followed his pointing finger, thinking of all the history built into this region. Then she sighed. "It feels sad here."

"Sad? With all this festivity going on around us? What's sad about it?"

"Because it's a place of survival. I can see people and animals dying out there because they didn't know water was close by. Or people traveling so far from home and barely making it to the pools. I don't know . . . it just feels sad to me."

A somber refrain from her days in church floated murkily to Cleo's mind: "By the waters of Babylon, there we sat down and wept." She couldn't remember the rest of the poem, but she thought it was a psalm.  Something about willow trees and harps.  *I'll look it up in that little Bible I carried on my wedding day,* she thought.

All day long the older boys had chased each other with firecrackers, and their irritating pops were constant.  But at sundown, the real fireworks began, spectacular against the blackness of the great vaulted sky.

It was late when the events of the day wound down.  Some would be going to town to spend the night, while others—like the Kinneys—had planned to camp out among the willows and start back for their homes in the morning.

Cleo lay awake on her quilt under the starry heavens, long after Tom was snoring beside her.  Funny how these same stars were shining over Houston just as they were here.  The same God she had learned about in Sunday school had made them.  But the stars seemed brighter out here, bigger, almost close enough to touch.  God, too, seemed nearer . . . almost close enough to touch, she thought just before she drifted off into a dreamless sleep.

## nine

A few days later, noticing Tom's restlessness and irritability, Cleo questioned him about it.

"It's time for the loan to come due," he said with a defeated sigh. "I'm so tired of scratching out a living on this place. If only it would rain, things would ease up. Joneses are leaving. They can't make it."

She held her breath. "Are you thinking of leaving, too?"

"Not until I don't have any other choices."

"Tom, it doesn't have to be this hard," she said quietly. "I have money. Father has money. There's no shame in letting someone help you." She snuggled against him in their feather bed. "Consider it as loan. You could pay it back in time."

He looked down into the deep pools of her smoky blue eyes. "You should know me well enough by now to know I can't do that."

She was careful with her next question. "Tom, would you let me and the baby suffer because of your pride?"

He recoiled. "Are you suffering? I thought you were happy here with me."

"Of course, I am!" she reassured him. "And I'm not really suffering. It *is* hard, but that's because I've never known what it was to work for a living. Father always had money, but I never saw him earn it. The point is, if you'd let me help you, we could have a nice home out here. Be comfortable. Have the things we needed. You could concentrate on building, not just holding things together."

Recognizing the wisdom of her words, he didn't answer her right away. She was right. He shouldn't be scraping and clawing, he should be improving the ranch. But if he took the money, his manhood would be in question. He had to prove—at least to himself—that he could make it on his own the way his father had, and his father before him.

As if reading his thoughts, Cleo spoke up. "I don't think people would look down on you. Your father and grandfather had their own ways of making money. If by marrying me, you came into some, then that's just another way of making it. And heaven knows, being married to me, you've earned every cent of it!"

He chuckled and pulled her even closer. "Let me think it over, honey. I've never been one to jump on the first train."

"You jumped quickly enough on my train."

"Yeah, but I could see it was first-class all the way."

Their laughter drained away the tension from between them, and curled together, they slept like innocent children.

Cleo didn't speak of the money to Tom for the next few days, but she could tell he was thinking about the matter.

Once again, waiting until they were snuggled in their bed after the others had retired for the night, he broached the subject. "I've given a lot of thought to what you said." He sighed deeply and with a hint of resignation. "I guess my pride will have to take a back seat to my common sense. I can't stand by and see you work so hard. And I don't want to lose the ranch. So I'll take you up on your offer to use your money . . . but I promise you, you'll get it back, with interest!"

It was all Cleo could do to restrain her squeal of delight. "Oh, Tom, you won't regret this! But you do realize that this makes me part owner in the ranch, don't you?"

"I guess it does. Well, partner, if you agree, I'd like to begin by paying off the mortgage on the ranch, so we can own our place, free and clear. Then we'll see where we are."

She grinned at him broadly. "There's something else I haven't told you."

He eyed her with suspicion. "And that is . . .?"

"When I'm twenty-five, I come into my trust fund." She paused to give him time to think. "That's about a million and some change." She laughed loudly at the astonishment on his face.

His gasp of astonishment let her know that she had taken him completely by surprise.

"I didn't tell you, because I was afraid I'd scare you off."

"And you never said a word." He shook his head, still not believing his ears. "I knew you'd get something when your father died, but I never dreamed about any kind of trust fund. No wonder he was so protective." His mind was reeling with all the possibilities of her disclosure. "I never dreamed," he breathed again.

A tiny breath of frosty fear stirred in Cleo's heart as her husband's delight grew. She moved against him, seeking reassurance, as the fears of her childhood echoed in her mind. "This doesn't change anything. We're still the same people. Money is just money."

Tom heard the raw need in her voice. "Honey, if I had known about your money before I knew you, it might have changed things between us," he said gently. "But I knew the real you. I love the real you. The money means that things will be easier for us, that's all." And his kiss sealed the bargain.

But in spite of his reassurances, for the next few days Cleo watched Tom for signs of change. She thought she noticed subtle differences—maybe he was a little too quick to pull out a chair for her, or he took her arm a bit too readily—and then was ashamed of her suspicions.

She wrote to her family, asking her father to transfer the remainder of her bank account to the bank in Wink, telling him that she wanted to pay off the loan on the ranch. It was a cheerful letter, describing the picnic on the dunes and her meeting with an oil speculator. Once again she mentioned the plan to come for a visit after her child was born. "If it is a girl, I want to call her Claire," she wrote, "but her full name would be Madeline Claire, for you, Mother."

The Seachrists had been spending more and more time in their sitting room off the bedroom, lounging before the fireplace which was now filled with potted plants for the summer. The deepening wrinkles on Madeline's face bore mute testimony to the worries she had endured since her daughter's marriage. And Henry looked much thinner, almost frail. He was grateful to be alive, but deeply grieved by the letter he was holding in his hand.

"It's starting, Henry, just as we feared," Madeline said softly.

"Now, Mother, it may not be as bad as we think." He tried to comfort her. "The rest of her letter is quite cheerful."

Madeline's concern thrust her from the chair into a restless pacing. "Our daughter is married to a man we don't know, is living in the wilderness, and is going to have her first child! Now we learn that she has obviously not been telling us everything that's going on. Why does she need the money?"

Scanning the letter over the glasses perched on the end of his nose, he looked up. "She says it's to pay off the loan on the ranch. Doesn't sound as if she's going hungry to me. Sounds like a firm business deal."

While Madeline fretted about Cleo's latest revelation, Henry was trying to decide how to tell his family that things weren't going too well for him financially. With his ill health, he hadn't been able to oversee his business. The market was in a slump, and several of his deals had gone sour. If things continued on this track, it was possible that he wouldn't be able to support their current life-style for long, unless he borrowed on his life insurance.

He was still thinking about it later that night as he eased to the edge of sleep in the sumptuous bedroom, though he didn't pray about it. Prayer was reserved for the dignity of the stately church service on Sunday morning. Intelligent men knew God didn't interfere in the business world. That world was a dice throw. Henry wondered how long his luck would last. And if it would get better . . . or worse.

The letter Cleo held in her hand was rather brief and straight-forward. Her father had laid it on the line. He was unable to send the money she requested, vaguely alluding to some "problems" with the business. He recommended she come home immediately, with no apology for failing to grant her request. Cleo was utterly confused. What about her bank account? Her house? Obviously her father didn't want to share any of this with her yet. But why?

She turned her shocked face to a tight-lipped Tom. "I don't understand. What shall I do?"

"*I* get it," he said through clenched teeth. "Your father doesn't trust me. He thinks all I ever wanted from you was your money . . . and his. This is his way of making sure I don't get my hands on any of it." Tom's face, bronzed from the sun, was now flushed with anger.

Cleo kept silent, wondering whether she should try to defend her father, and the tiny doubt about Tom's love for her coiled and rattled in the corner of her mind. Hearing no denial of his accusations, Tom stomped from the house to the barn, where he saddled his horse and rode off into the darkness to cool off.

Mrs. Kinney came out of her bedroom. From the look of

condemnation on her face, it was clear that she had heard the entire conversation. Without a word to Cleo, she lit the kerosene lantern and walked outside to hang it high on the windmill next to the house, lighting her son's way back.

But Tom didn't return until well after dawn. And when Cleo came in for breakfast, Tom was sitting at the table with a cup of steaming coffee in his hand, his mother stirring a pan of grits.

"Tom, can we talk about this in private?" Cleo asked quietly. She heard a soft "Hrumph!" from the vicinity of the stove, but ignored it. Tom took his coffee and headed out the back door for the shade of the old mulberry tree. Then, leaning with his back against it, he waited for her to speak.

"What do you want me to do?" she asked.

"What do you want to do?" he countered. "I don't think going back there will help anything. But it's obviously where he wants you . . . away from me. Maybe he's right." Tom peered into the endless prairie as if to read the future. "Maybe you'd better get out while you still can. It's obvious I can't take care of you like your daddy can."

Her silent tears traced a path down her cheeks. "Tom, I don't want to leave you. I love you and my place is here with you. I'm sorry I got your hopes up for the ranch. I honestly thought I could help." She walked over and eased her bulk beside him, leaning into the broadness of his chest. "Please tell me you don't want me to leave." Her smoky blue eyes were enormous in her pinched face.

Tom leaned down and gently placed his lips over hers. "Stay with me," he whispered into her hair. "I don't ever want you to leave me. You know I need you, with or without your money." He smoothed back her hair, and they sealed their pledges to one another with another kiss while Mrs. Kinney watched shamelessly from the kitchen window.

In the next few days Cleo gave a great deal of thought to the letter she was writing to her parents. She was working on the final draft when Robert burst into the kitchen where she was sitting at the table. "Wire for you, Cleo!"

With hands that trembled, she reached for the envelope, opened it, and read silently. "Oh, no . . . no!" she cried brokenly. Telegram dangling from her hand, she walked out to their bedroom in the new wing and sat down on the bed.

Mrs. Kinney wasn't far behind. "Bad news?" she asked, wiping her hands on her damp apron.

"Where's Tom?" Cleo said dully, ignoring her mother-in-law's question. "I want Tom."

"Robert, go get Tom and bring him here." Mrs. Kinney took one look at Cleo's ashen face and hurried to get her a glass of water. Clumsily she pushed the water into Cleo's numb hand and guided the glass to her lips. Then she retreated to the living room to wait for her son. She could hear her daughter-in-law's soft sobs, but she made no attempt to go comfort the girl. That was her son's job.

Tom rushed into the house and headed straight for his weeping wife. "What is it, honey?"

"Oh, Tom, he's dead! Father's dead! Why didn't they tell me he was so sick? I didn't know. The letter must have been his way of asking me to come home before it was too late. Oh, why didn't I go?"

Tom made soothing noises and stroked her hair, holding her close while she wailed her guilt and remorse.

There was no discussing whether she would go back home for her father's funeral. She started packing right away. Pregnant or not, she was needed at home. And she needed to be there. However, it was decided that Tom would not make the trip with her.

Traveling over the sand was a trial, but it was the easy

part of the journey. The train ride seemed to take forever, and its constant lurching and swaying made Cleo sick. In her car she tried to breathe through thick cigar fumes, plotting revenge on the insensitive old goat who alternately smoked and chewed the awful weed.

Her mother met her at the station, and the familiar ritual began to unfold.

The funeral was orchestrated to bring comfort to the grieving family, with many of Houston's most prominent families attending. In public, her mother was stalwart and strong. But it was only after all the mourners had left at last and the maid had cleared the huge dining room table of the food brought in by friends that Madeline invited her daughter up to her room to talk privately.

"It was a lovely service, don't you think, dear? I love the way the Reverend Kohl preaches. And so many people. My, I knew we had a lot of friends, but I never realized how many until I saw the full church today. It's quite a tribute to your father." Madeline sipped a cup of coffee and threaded her way carefully through the first acknowledged day of her widowhood.

Cleo recognized the reddened eyes, faded mirrors of her own, and replied with the correct responses to her mother's monologue.

"And the reading of the will tomorrow, of course. I don't think there will be many surprises." Madeline Seachrist took another sip of coffee and leaned back in her chaise lounge, running her fingers lightly around the rim of the bone china cup. Time seemed to be softening the edges of her immediate grief and taking her back to the happy days.

Cleo listened to her mother reminisce and watched with some concern as she let down her guard. But Cleo's attention was jerked sharply into focus at her mother's next words.

"I should say that there won't be any surprises for *me*

tomorrow . . . but I must prepare you . . . " Madeline paused and watched Cleo anxiously. "I think it's all gone . . . the money, I mean. Henry would never tell me the whole truth. When he refused to send you the money you asked for, I knew something was wrong, for he has never denied you anything. When I questioned him, he admitted to some trouble with the cash flow, but I could tell that things were worse than he was letting on."

She shook her head and laughed sadly. "Men are so silly about not wanting to worry us, and then they die and we have to put everything together again." She walked over to the mantel, fingering the ornately carved molding. "I think I'll sell the house and move into something . . . cozier. Without Henry . . ." Madeline broke off, her eyes filling with quick tears—"this place will feel so empty."

She turned to regard Cleo sadly. "It was all for you, anyway. You were the only reason we needed money. I wanted to give you everything. To make you happy. To give you the kind of life you deserved."

Cleo made soft protests, but her mother continued. "I loved you from the first moment I thought of you. I was so happy we would have our little girl."

"And how could you be so sure I would be a girl?" Cleo asked curiously.

Her mother paused only a moment, then drew up her shoulders with resolution. "A long time before I met your father, I was in love with a man . . . a boy, really." She sighed. "I was young and ignorant, and I thought he loved me, too. When he found out about the baby, he took the first road out of town. My parents sent me back East to stay with my aunt until the child came." She began to weep as Cleo's face crumpled in disbelief. "Don't hate me, darling. Please don't hate me."

"What happened to . . . that baby?" Cleo's voice was

strangled with emotion.

"I gave it up. My aunt took her to an orphanage." She looked pitifully into Cleo's eyes. "I couldn't take care of a child, darling. I had no choice."

Cleo heard her mother's confession with horror. Horror at the deception her mother had revealed to her, pity for the ordeal she had endured. Carefully and lovingly she gathered her weeping mother into her arms. "You didn't have to tell me this now, Mother. It makes no difference."

"But there's more." Madeline Kinney moved away to compose herself. Then, looking at the daughter she loved so desperately, she drew a deep breath, knowing that her next words would change Cleo's life forever.

# ten

"I never got over the guilt of giving my little girl away," Madeline went on. "I never stopped thinking of her. Your father was a kind and loving man, but I never tested his love by telling him about my child. Her birth was difficult, and when we wanted to have children, I wasn't able to conceive. When it appeared that we could not have children of our own, I decided to help someone else's child, the way I hoped someone had helped mine. It wasn't hard to talk your father into an adoption."

Cleo felt fear tighten her stomach and a denial sprang to her lips, though she did not utter it. *No, no, don't tell me this! I don't want to hear it!*

"I read in the papers that New York City was crowded with children of all ages. They were to be loaded on trains and sent throughout the rural parts of the country."

"You mean the Orphan Trains?" Cleo was horrified.

"Yes." Madeline smoothed her dressing gown. "The same Baby Trains we have today."

Cleo could feel the room beginning to spin.

Her mother quietly continued her story. "Oh, I didn't do as some did—wait until the train stopped and the children were lined up on the depot platform. I wrote to the same orphanage where I had left my child and asked specifically for a baby girl. For *you*." Her eyes filled with unshed tears. "Your father and I ordered you . . . like a doll from a catalog."

Cleo could see her mother leave the present as she relived the past. "I got a reply from the orphanage very quickly.

You were a newborn—black hair, blue eyes, of course, and the most exquisite skin. White like milk. And a baby bud of a mouth." She turned and looked at Cleo. "I'm sure your father would have preferred a son, but I was so insistent on a daughter that he didn't have the heart to oppose me. And I loved you from the moment I sent off the letter.

"The day the train was due, I thought we would never get to the station. We knew you would be accompanied by a woman from the orphanage, so we looked for her." Sadness strained Madeline's face as she remembered the scene. "It was awful. Children and babies everywhere—crying, confused, being inspected like cattle at an auction. Some would choose a child, separating him from his brothers and sisters. Farmers selected the oldest and strongest ones to work on their farms. Others, like you, were chosen in love.

"When I found you at last, tagged with our name, I thought I would die of happiness. You were my little girl come back to me."

Cleo knew of the baby trains, but they were seldom mentioned in polite company. An open secret that no one wanted to acknowledge. The idea had seemed like a good one at first, but it had grown ugly over the years. And now her own mother was telling her that she was one of those orphans! *This is a nightmare,* she decided. Maybe she would wake up.

But when she opened her eyes, her mother was standing before her, tears raining down her cheeks, washing away the years of guilt, and in her confession, destroying forever the security Cleo had always known.

Cleo couldn't bear any more revelations. "Come, let me put you down to sleep now, Mother. You'll feel better after you rest."

Madeline didn't resist, but willingly allowed Cleo to tuck her into bed. And in the stillness of her girlhood bedroom,

Cleo tried to deal with all that she had learned. It was too much to comprehend. Grief over the loss of her father and her mother's admission rolled over her like a huge green ocean wave, drowning her in its depths.

Cleo's child woke her in the morning with a rollicking bounce. It was a now familiar sensation, but when she opened her eyes and looked around, she knew she was not in her bed at the ranch.

A giant fist slammed into her middle as she remembered the events of the day before, and she felt as if she were choking. *I'm not really their daughter. I'm not part of them. It was all a charade.* And she wept tears of desolation. She had lost her father who wasn't really her father, and her mother had picked her out of an orphanage. *Who am I?* she cried.

Exhausted from her restless night, Cleo went into the luxurious bathroom and ran a tub of hot water. Easing her bulk down into the fragrant bubbles, she soaked for a long time, thinking of the news she had heard.

Still feeling numb, she toweled herself dry, dressed, and went downstairs to the dining room to face her mother who wasn't really her mother.

When Cleo entered the room, Madeline rose and enfolded her in a warm embrace. "I wasn't sure you'd come down today, darling." Cleo lost no time in getting to the point as she took her seat at the table, feeling the warming rays of sunlight streaming through the tall English windows. "Mother, why did you tell me? Why now?"

"The timing may not have been best," Madeline admitted, "but I felt you had the right to know the truth. It's possible someday you would have found out anyway, and I would rather you hear it from me."

They nibbled their toast in silence, each absorbing the

finality of recent events. "Have you ever wondered what happened to your . . . other daughter?" Cleo asked at last.

Madeline smiled sadly. "I think of her every year on her birthday. But it would serve no useful purpose for me to intrude on her life now. Besides, I have you. She's a closed chapter in my life." She hesitated. "But what about you . . . do you want to know about your real mother?"

Cleo put down her coffee cup and stared at her. "You *are* my real mother!" she decided on the spot and swiped at her eyes. "And you know, Mother, you're an amazing woman. It took a lot of courage to tell me your story. I doubt that many women would have taken that risk."

Madeline sighed deeply. "The most important part of that story is that your father loved you and I love you. When you hold your child in your arms, you'll understand. But I've often thought that when one deliberately seeks out a child, perhaps it is even more precious."

Without another word, Cleo rose from her chair and enfolded the seated woman holding out her arms. They wept silently together, resealing their relationship on a new level. They had chosen one another. There was no need to return to yesterday.

"What time is the lawyer coming?" Cleo asked as she refilled their coffee cups.

"Around ten. I expect a few long-lost cousins, too," her mother said wryly. "I think they will be in for an unhappy surprise."

"It's gone? All of it?"

"I can't be sure, but I know I will have to make some major changes in my life. As you know, Henry didn't want to trouble me with his worries. Consequently, I worried alone. Men are such ninnies about their wives, don't you think?"

Cleo felt a new surge of understanding between them.

"Sometimes I think I've married a little boy," she agreed. "Will you be all right here?"

"Of course, dear. Believe it or not, I am quite strong and self sufficient." She gave her daughter a penetrating look. "And you? Tell me about life in West Texas."

Cleo made no further attempt to withhold anything from her mother. Her words rushed out in a torrent. "I love Tom desperately, but I can't abide his mother. We're poor as church mice, and likely to lose the ranch. I hate the dreary West Texas weather. But most of all I hate the sand. And I miss you terribly." Her eyes filled with tears as she concluded her grim recital.

"Then stay with me," Madeline said quickly. "Write Tom and tell him to come back here. He can find a job again. Let the old biddy run her sandy kingdom."

"I wish it were that easy." Cleo shifted uncomfortably in her chair. "I'm sure Tom loves me, but to tell the truth, I'm not sure how much. The ranch means more to him than I realized. It seems to be all tied up with his male ego. And you know how big that is!" she added humorously.

"We'll work on this problem at tea time. I'll think about it and by then we'll know for sure what our financial picture is. As my mother used to say, 'It'll all come out in the wash.'" Madeline patted Cleo's hand and rose to face her new world.

Later that day, in the ornate room where Tom had asked for Cleo's hand, Madeline served the tea as gracefully as she had for the past thirty-five years. Her hand was steady and her voice clear and firm. "Now," she said as she settled back into the deep cushion of her chair with her own cup, "let's make some plans. I've already arranged with the lawyer to put this house on the market. And the realtor is searching for an appropriate apartment or small house for me. I've given the servants their notice." She paused, looking out the richly hung window, "You know, I'm rather looking forward to starting a new life in a new place. I think staying here would be harder for me with all its memories. I've arranged my life. Now, what shall we do about yours?"

"I can see only two options. Go or stay," Cleo said miserably. She looked toward her mother hopefully.

"Oh, no, my darling, you have to make this decision on your own. The only thing I can tell you is that nothing is forever. You can make a decision for now and, as things change, you can alter your plans. Just listen to your heart."

Cleo thought about that. It sounded like something Tante Olga might have said, though her mother had not mentioned God or prayer. Suddenly an overwhelming desire to run into Tom's arms swept over her. All else paled next to her need to be with him.

Her mother smiled. "I can see by the expression on your face what you've decided. I'll help you pack." She embraced Cleo. "I think you've made a good choice. And after I'm settled and feeling up to it, I may even come out west and give that old witch a run for her money."

Cleo's accompanying laugh was the happiest sound Madeline had heard in a long while.

As Cleo was putting her things in the traveling cases, she heard the phone ring and ran to answer it.

"Cleo!" came a familiar voice. "J.J. and I just got back from Bermuda. I'm just devastated about your father's death. I'm so sorry I wasn't there when you needed me. Are you all right? Can I come over now?" Mattie ran on, not pausing for breath.

"I'm fine, and yes, I'd love to see you right this minute."

"I'm on my way!"

It was like old times. The laughing and crying were pitched high and girlish, though the hugging was a little more long distance with Cleo's child between them.

"I'm jealous," Mattie admitted as they went into Cleo's bedroom. "J.J. and I would love to have a baby, too."

Cleo wrinkled her nose. "It's not what it's cracked up to be," she warned, "especially the first few weeks."

"Going back already?" Mattie asked when she saw the open suitcases.

"Yes. Tom is expecting me tomorrow."

They pushed the cases off the bed and curled up as they had in earlier, more carefree days. Cleo told Mattie the whole story while Mattie listened with astonishment, scarcely breathing throughout the entire monologue.

"Well?" Cleo demanded when she had come to the end of her tale. "Aren't you going to say something?"

"I—I don't know what to say," Mattie sputtered. "For the first time in my life, I'm speechless." Her lashes with laced with tears. "All I know is that you're still the dearest friend I have in the world. I've missed you and didn't know how much until I saw you again today. Do you really have to leave tomorrow?"

Cleo nodded firmly. "Things were very tense when I left. I want to go back and make sure Tom knows I love him and want to be with him." On impulse, she gave Mattie a conspiratorial glance. "Come with me."

"What?!" Mattie was aghast. "I can't come with you! I'm a married lady now. J.J. would have a fit." She paused. "For how long?"

"As long or as short a visit as you like."

"Would I have to share a room with Mrs. Kinney?"

Cleo went along with the mischievous look in her friend's eyes. "No, you can sleep out in the barn where it's safe."

Mattie sobered. "Are you serious . . . about my coming, I mean? Since it isn't your house . . ."

Cleo drew herself up importantly. "Remember, we've just

built an addition to the house. I can invite anybody I please. Besides," she went on, suddenly serious, "I need you, Mattie. It would mean a lot to me to have you there when the baby comes, especially since Mother can't come out until the estate is settled."

"Well, J.J. *is* working on an oil deal night and day. That's one reason we went to Bermuda. Maybe he'd appreciate my being out of his hair for a while." The sparkle in Mattie's eyes matched Cleo's.

On the train the next day, the two women talked all the way. Cleo tried to prepare Mattie for the experience. "You know we live on a real working ranch," she explained. "It's nothing fancy. No indoor plumbing . . . no running hot water . . . that sort of thing."

Mattie sighed. "Oh, I know you've said it's rustic, but it all sounds so terribly romantic."

"You won't think it's so romantic when you have to use the privy in the middle of the night. Did I mention to be careful of the black widow spiders that like to hide under the seat?"

"Oh, Cleo," Mattie wailed, "now you'll have to go with me!" And Cleo laughed as Tom had laughed at her introduction to ranch life.

They spoke of the coming baby and the small layette Cleo had assembled. Privately Mattie planned what she might do to make Cleo's life easier. But the more she heard about her friend's spartan existence, the more she disliked Tom Kinney. It was all his fault that Cleo was suffering! And she deliberately refused to think about Mrs. Kinney until she was forced to deal with Cleo's mother-in-law face to face.

Cleo had wired Tom to meet her, but had not mentioned that Mattie would be coming, too. She noticed with relief that he covered his shock well, and she concentrated on demonstrating to him how much she had missed him.

Tom, on the other hand, was quietly resentful. His greeting to Mattie was cordial, but restrained. *That's all I need now,* he thought, *reinforcements for her side.* But he knew alienating Mattie wouldn't help his cause, so he was carefully deferential.

Mattie amused them with her naive remarks as they jounced along the road to the ranch. Both Tom and Cleo were happy to postpone the exchange of any serious news and pointed out the landmarks along the way.

At the ranch, Robert gallantly gave up his room and even Mrs. Kinney was civil to her houseguest, though her sharp eyes were taking in every detail of Mattie's attire. In those faded eyes, Cleo could read the same disapproval she herself had received from her those months ago.

After Mattie was settled, Cleo went back to her own retreat where she knew Tom would be waiting for her.

Silently he took her in his arms. "I missed you like crazy," he breathed against her mouth. "Promise me you won't ever go away again."

She pulled away to look up into his dark eyes. "I was afraid you'd never speak to me again. You were so formal at the train depot."

"I was surprised to see Mattie, that's all. I thought maybe you had brought her in for reinforcements." He smiled a lazy smile. "But when you wouldn't let go of my hand all the way home, I knew you weren't mad at me." To demonstrate how glad he was to see her, he kissed her long and lovingly.

"Guess we were both wrong." Cleo gently disengaged herself from his embrace and began taking off her traveling clothes. "I have so much to tell you. So very much."

Pulling on a wrapper, she perched on their bed and

considered how best to break the news. "First of all, there isn't any money. I'm sorry. Father wasn't being mean, he was just broke. And Mother is selling the house and moving into an apartment. She'll have only enough money to take care of herself." She looked intently into her husband's face. "What are we going to do?"

Tom plowed his hands through his hair, taking time to assimiliate the information. "I don't know, but I'll think of something. I hadn't counted on your money to begin with, you know."

She wanted to tell him about the orphan train, but he seemed so distracted that she didn't have the heart to dump any more on him. What could he do about it anyway? It didn't change things between them. Or did it? She wasn't ready to find out.

"I'm planning to ship some cattle. Maybe I'll ship more than I planned." He looked at her rounded figure lovingly. "Don't you worry, honey. You just take care of that baby of ours."

She took him at his word. With the baby coming, there was a lot to think about. And if Tom lost the ranch, would that really be such a tragedy? After all, it would mean they that could go back to Houston. And after seeing "civilization" again, West Texas now looked like the end of the world. She began to have serious doubts about having a baby in this forsaken place. *What if something goes wrong?*

The thought persisted over the next few days, and each kick of the baby was a reminder of her fear. And then she remembered what Tante Olga had said about depending on God each day and began to pray. *Lord, I don't have any control over what happens to me and the baby. Please keep us both safe. And thank You for Mattie. I know she's an answer to my prayers. I haven't always been faithful to You, and I've been careless with all the blessings You've*

*given me. But as I grow older and wiser and live in this
land, I know I can't make it without You.* A lump had risen
in her throat at her confession of her need for the Lord, and
she knew that she had come a long way since her Sunday
school days. Her prayers were no longer girlish babble, but
the deep heart cries of a grown woman.

Mattie never complained about the lack of amenities on the
ranch, but it was plain that each day was a surprise to her.
And when they took her to a dance over at Crook's place,
she chatted with everyone there and danced the night away,
while Cleo sat on the sidelines and drank gallons of tea.

On the way home in the stillness of the night, she told
Cleo, "I don't think I ever met a nicer bunch of people.
Quaint, but nice. Living out here sure changes one's point
of view, doesn't it?"

Cleo laughed. "Yes. Life seems completely different out
here. Sometimes I hate it," she said softly so Tom couldn't
hear her, "but the people make it bearable."

"*Most* of them anyway," whispered Mattie, and she cut
her eyes to the dour Mrs. Kinney as they both suppressed a
soft giggle.

# eleven

Tom made the next mortgage payment with a large shipment of cattle. It was a disappointment to see his herd growing smaller, but there was nothing else to be done. Once, when Mattie tried to approach him about the wildcatting J.J. was doing, he cut her off with a surly retort before she could finish her sentence.

Near the end of Cleo's pregnancy, the two women were sitting under the tree in the back yard, sipping lemonade and enjoying the cooling fall breeze.

Cleo watched Mattie scanning the horizon. "You're getting bored, aren't you." It was more statement than question.

Her friend turned to her with a sigh. "A little, though being with you is rarely boring. But I do miss J.J."

"And parties and restaurants and plays and . . . life," added Cleo lightly. "So do I."

"You'll soon have your hands full with your little one."

"The sooner the better. I'm so uncomfortable I'd walk barefoot through hot coals to get this lump off my front."

"I still think you should move into Midland. If it's a matter of money, I'd like to . . ." Mattie began carefully.

A sudden look of alarm crossed Cleo's face. "Oh, Mattie, I think it may be too late to go anywhere. I think the baby is coming . . . now!"

Mattie helped her into the house and called Mrs. Kinney and Tom.

"Cleo, honey, what do you want me to do?" he asked.

"Go get Tante Olga. She promised she'd come. I need

136

her, Tom."

"I'll get her, honey. Don't worry." Tom glared at his mother. "I know you can take care of things while I'm gone, Ma."

She nodded silently and went into the kitchen to put on the coffeepot.

When Olga arrived, she found Cleo dressed primly in a white cotton gown and tucked into bed. Tom was sent away to occupy himself with chores while the women got down to work.

As her labor progressed, Cleo said, "I wish I were at home." This escalated to "I wish I'd never married that man!" Finally, her wail blossomed to "I never should have come to this place with that man!"

"I know how you feel," observed Tante Olga.

"Not unless you've had a baby, you don't!" Cleo shot back tartly.

"I've had six." She wiped Cleo's forehead. "Vhen I first come to America, I vas so frightened. I don't speak the language even. Den I marry and come here and vas *really* frightened!" She laughed. "I remember a psalm. I read it many times."

> By the rivers of Babylon we sat and wept
>    when we remembered Zion.
> There on the willow trees
>    we hung our harps,
> for there our captors asked us for songs,
>    our tormentors demanded songs of joy;
> How can we sing the songs of the Lord
>    while in a foreign land?

"Dis out here is, for sure, a foreign land." She fussed around Cleo. "But soon you vill think of it as your home, not a foreign land. And you vill love your husband again. More than ever." Her eyes twinkled with good humor.

As another contraction hit Cleo, she had the gravest of doubts. "And where is my loving husband now?" she moaned.

"Soon. He vill be here soon," crooned Tante Olga.

Tom and Mattie were keeping vigil outside, but the sounds of Cleo's deepening labor could be clearly heard. They comforted one another with assurances neither fully believed.

Mattie moved between Tom and Cleo as the time drew nearer for their child to be delivered. So it was her good fortune to announce to Tom the arrival of his baby daughter. "Hale and hearty, with blue eyes like her mother and hair like yours!" she cried delightedly.

Cleo named the baby for her mother, as she had promised, and the days went by in a blur as she cared for the infant. Each day she thanked the Lord for her beautiful daughter. And Tom, being a dutiful father, hid any disappointment he might have felt in not having a son.

He also hid their deepening financial pit. He had ridiculed Mattie's suggestions about drilling for oil on his land, but with news of a big oil strike in Pecos again, he found himself reconsidering. It would mean quick money if he hit oil. *If.*

A few days later Robert came riding up to the ranch, yelling for Tom. His mount was hard-ridden and Robert's eyes were glassy with wonder. "They did it! Old man Hendricks has struck it rich! The whole town's gone wild. The place is crawlin' with men and machines. Promoters, drillers, tool dressers, gamblers and ladies of the night! It's like a circus. Money is flowin' like water!"

"Whoa. Slow down. You mean in Kermit?"

"You wouldn't even recognize the place," Robert told him. "Tent houses have sprouted like mushrooms in a good rain. Buildings made of anythin' people can get their hands on!"

Tom shook his head and tried to picture sleepy little Kermit as Robert had described it. "I've got to see for myself."

Tom and Robert could hear the ruckus long before they rode into town. In a very short time, the place had been overrun with blocks and blocks of hastily constructed shops. It seemed all the trades and services were represented. Tom didn't like the looks of some of the men he saw scurrying by. And there were attractive women whose eyes were not shy when they looked at a man.

It was in the midst of this hullabaloo that he spotted Leaf entering a brand-new mercantile. It had been a long time since they had chatted, and he hurried to catch up with her.

"Leaf!" he called, seeing her pause along a planked wood counter. "Leaf, it's been a long time." When she turned to face him, he was shocked to see the change in her appearance. It seemed that she was wearing too much makeup, and her dress was cut so low that he willed himself to keep his gaze glued to her face.

"Hi, Tom. What do you think of our new town? Exciting, isn't it?" Her eyes held an unmistakeable challenge.

"And I see you've changed your style to fit the big city."

She shrugged. "I got tired of cowboys who never had time for anything but cows. The men here are very interesting."

"What does your father have to say about that?"

"I wouldn't know. I have my own place now. I share it with another girl."

"Do you have a job?" he asked, hoping he was wrong in his suspicions.

Her chin went up defiantly. "You might say that. The shopowners aren't too thrilled with me, but they take my money. And I have quite a lot of it. It's an easy job, and I make my own hours."

Tom's eyes dropped to the tips of his boots. "Leaf . . ."

"Don't say anything, Tom. I think I was meant for this kind of life. It sure beats being a secretary for my father. I like the money. I like the freedom. And I meet some really nice men." She regarded him steadily. "But I hope I can still talk to some of my old friends."

"We go back a long way."

"*Too* long. That was one of the problems." She laughed again. "I see Robert over there. Say hello to him for me. Guess he's too shy to talk to me right now."

"Be happy," Tom said softly, and tipped his hat to her.

"Is she all right?" Robert asked when Tom rejoined him.

"*She* thinks so. How long has she been . . . in town?"

"How should I know?" Robert spread his hands innocently.

"I think you know more than you let on. What else have you been finding out in town?"

Robert was belligerent. "Talking to some promoters."

"About what?" Tom asked through clenched teeth.

"Leasing our land. For drilling. They'd make us a real good deal, Tom. And if they hit oil, we'd be rich!"

Tom could hear the greed in his brother's voice, but with the idea of quick money staring him in the face, he would be stupid not to hear more. His ranch was still in danger.

When they picked up the mail, there was a letter from J.J. to Mattie, and that reminded Tom of J.J.'s offer to stake him in a business venture. Oil was swirling all around in his brain, but he couldn't shake the feeling he was betraying all his ranching heritage if he succumbed. Could he use the one to support the other? If he got oil-rich, he could make the ranch into the dream he had for it. He shook his head to clear his mind. But the idea wouldn't die as he rode back to the ranch.

Robert was sullen and silent, still chafing from his brother's rebuke, as they rode along in the soft sand. Tom's eyes wandered across the vastness of the range to the blue horizon. *What should I do, Lord?* he asked. *You gave us all this land for the cattle. Is this oil thing Your way of helping me get the ranch going again? Tell me what to do.* He sighed as he walked his horse toward the barn and waited for an answer.

Mattie met the letter from J.J. with a delighted squeal and retreated to her bedroom to read it privately. In a few minutes she let out a loud "Whoopee!" and came tearing out of the room waving the letter. "J.J.'s coming! He'll be here in less than a week. Seems news of the strike has reached all the way to Houston." Her eyes danced with happiness.

J.J.'s arrival was cause for a celebration. There was a lot of catching up on news, the baby to admire, and the local boom to discuss. Robert was full of information, and Tom listened. Later during a lull, Tom and J.J. drifted to the back yard.

"So, how will all this affect your ranching, Tom?" asked J.J., looking prosperous and up to date. Tom felt like a handyman beside him.

"Depends," he replied noncommittally.

"Up to you, you know, whether you cash in on it or not." J.J. took a deep drag on his expensive cigar. The smoke ring rose around his head, and he stroked his newly-grown mustache with a well manicured hand.

"I know you love your wife, J.J., but I have the feeling this is really a business trip." Tom laughed softly.

"You are an astute man. Are you as good a businessman?"

"How do we do this?"

"I put up the capital, you provide the land. And labor, of course. I'd want you to be there to supervise the whole thing."

"I don't know the first thing about drilling an oil well."

"You'll learn quickly. And we'll hire good men." He took another puff. "Before you know it, we'll both be oil men." He winked happily.

"Just that easy?"

"Yep. I've seen it happen many times before."

Tom was skeptical. "Hmm. What happens if there isn't any oil on this land?"

"There's oil in Pecos and there's oil on the Hendricks's ranch, and you're sitting squarely in between. How can we miss?"

"It's tempting. But I swore I'd never drill on my land."

"It takes a smart man to change his mind when the facts change," J.J. said smoothly. "Besides, what alternatives do you have?"

"None I can think of." Tom chuckled. "But I don't want to go into this thing by default."

"Not by default, my friend. By choice. You'll choose to make us both very rich." He smiled a wide smile at Tom. "Deal?"

Tom matched J.J.'s firm handshake. "Deal." He shook his head. "But I'm not sure what I'm getting myself into."

J.J. clapped him on the back. "A brand-new world, my friend, a brand-new world."


J.J. went into town the next day with Tom as a very silent partner. J.J. did all the wheeling and dealing. He hired men for a drilling crew while Tom nodded an affirmative once in a while on his choice of workers.

The most important decision they had to make was where

to drill. Using a map, J.J. drew a line straight from Pecos to the Hendricks strike. He pointed, grinning, to where it crossed Tom's land. "That's the honey hole."

With the help of a man who claimed to be a geologist, the spot was confirmed and they were ready to drill.

The news had been met by Mrs. Kinney first with rage, then with grudging acceptance. She retreated more and more from the family, muttering dire predictions under her breath. Had they not all been so busy—Cleo with the baby and Tom with his new venture—they would have noticed that she was fading from the world. But everyone was too busy to take time for a bitter old woman.

Tom was out at the drilling site day and night, taking two "towers" a day, as the shifts were called. Robert made himself a camp on the site, and J.J. often stayed in town to oversee the business end of things.

"I thought this was going to be good for all of us," complained Cleo to Mattie.

"Did I forget to mention what it's like to be married to a hotshot businessman?" she said with a wry look. "That's one of the reasons I knew J.J. wouldn't miss me too much if I came out here."

"Well, as soon as they hit the oil, things will change," Cleo consoled herself.

"Sure they will. Then they'll start on the second well, so they can be twice as rich. You don't understand that this is a sickness. And it only gets worse."

"Then I hope they don't strike," Cleo said adamantly.

Mattie laughed. "Oh, that won't change anything. Once the fever takes hold of a man, he's hooked. We'll be oil widows no matter what."

Cleo felt a tingle of alarm. "I hope you're wrong. After all, Tom does have a family," she said hopefully.

"Maybe Tom will be different," suggested Mattie. "But

you can thank God every day you have little Claire."

To her prayers for her child, Cleo added some for Tom's new obsession. *Please don't let it change Tom,* she pleaded. *Help him keep his balance and let us be a happy family.*

The first well came in a duster. Cleo had never seen anyone as disappointed as Tom when he came in to tell her. But when she tried to console him, he pushed her away.

"I'm disappointed, of course, Cleo, but there's oil out there. I'm positive of it. You know when they were going to drill on the Hendricks's ranch, they chose the place and then tried to drag the drilling sled there. It got stuck in the deep sand before they ever reached the drill site, so they decided to drill right there. And that's where they hit it! If they'd drilled in the original place, they might have missed it altogether. That's the oil game. Exciting as all get-out." He took off his grimy shirt and pumped water into the kitchen sink, splashing it all over his head and upper body.

It had been too long since she'd snuggled next to that firm body. Drilling had taken her place in his heart for now. Every moment was dedicated to bringing in the oil. She turned away sadly.

He and J.J. sat up late and worked their way through the new drilling plans. J.J.'s father would put up the money for the next test well. But, he had warned, he'd go with only one well. If they hit another duster, they'd have to find other ways of financing the next venture.

"We'll get her this time, old pal," J.J. assured Tom.

"To Number Two," Tom said, lifting his water glass. "Two has always been my lucky number."

Mattie and Cleo went to their respective beds and listened to their men bragging and patting each other on the back until they fell asleep to its boring repetition.

On their husbands' orders, Mattie and Cleo hadn't ventured

into town. "A boom town is no place for a lady," they had told their wives. Which only made Cleo and Mattie more determined to see what they were missing. With the two men away so much and Mrs. Kinney keeping to herself in her room, they decided that they deserved a day out. Cleo had asked Tante Olga to keep Claire, and she and Mattie were like the young girls back in Galveston, getting ready for the adventure of Splash Day.

Cleo regarded her long dark hair in the mirror. "It looks so shaggy and so, well, country." She turned slowly and studied her image. "What happened to the chic society girl?"

Mattie laughed. "Oh, she's still there, somewhere under all that sand and hair."

Cleo's eyes widened. "Oh, Mattie, I just remembered a dream I had last night. I was standing outside this shanty overlooking the prairie with a baby in my arms and one dragging on my skirt, and I was pregnant with another child. I woke up crying, because I knew we were all hungry." She turned to Mattie. "It won't be like that, will it? Tell me it won't!"

"Never." She hugged Cleo and said, "Hurry up and get dressed. We're going to be 'beautified' today. My treat," she added firmly.

Cleo walked to the chifforobe and reached deep in the back. "I still have a little money of my own."

"Hmm, just think what damage the two of us can do!" laughed Mattie.

Cleo gasped when she saw Kermit in the distance. "This isn't a little town anymore. Look at all the people!"

"It looks more like Houston . . . the other side of the tracks, that is," Mattie said through gritted teeth as the buggy bounced over the ruts in the road. "Where did all those cars come from . . . and trucks . . . and isn't that an electrical line overhead?"

People were swarming all over the town like ants on a hill. Buying and selling of every sort was going on on every street corner, and the noise was like downtown Houston at rush hour. For a moment, Cleo thought she was dreaming.

"Where do you want to go first?" Mattie asked, jolting her out of her reverie.

"The beauty shop. Then a dress shop."

"What about this one?" Mattie said, eyeing a woman who had walked out of one little shop, patting her fresh coiffeur.

Inside, a beautician indicated a vacant chair. "I have room for one of you. Now, dearie, what can I do for you today?" she asked Cleo as she tied a large towel around her neck. Seeing Cleo's look of surprise as another patron—a flamboyantly dressed young woman—left the shop, she hastened to reassure her. "Oh, don't worry, we don't have too many of *that* kind in here. Besides, she's a pretty nice person, but I can't say much for her business practices, if you know what I mean. Oh, I can't afford to turn them away. They have most of the money in this town, you know, and they tip good. . . . Now, what's for you today?" She ran her hands through Cleo's ebony hair, lifting its weight from her neck.

"I want it cut in the latest fashion . . . whatever that is."

The operator laughed at Cleo's look of puzzlement. "Just leave it to me." And for the next hour, Cleo put herself in the woman's hands, while Mattie received a full beauty treatment in the adjoining chair.

Their ears grew bigger as they listened to the two beauty operators' talk in lowered tones. "The one who was just in here . . . you know? I hear Slim's taken a liking to her. Keeps his stooges off her back. She don't have to pay him no kickbacks as long as she keeps seein' him," said the one named Thelma.

"Yeah," Helen replied, "he's got this town locked up. Slim bein' the mayor and the police chief his partner, what sweeter deal could there be?"

They continued gossiping, giving away much of the town secrets to the two young women, who sat immobile in their chairs. And by the time they left the shop, Cleo and Mattie were well informed about the local news.

"Mattie," Cleo whispered outside the shop, "I wanted my hair done, but I'm glad I didn't spend any money on a permanent. Those stories curled my hair!"

Mattie glanced around nervously. "I had no idea all this was going on. No wonder the men didn't want us to come to town. Let's get our shopping over and get home."

On the way home at last, they welcomed the vast slab of land that curved out of sight before them, broken only by a few mesquite trees and stubby grass. At least it was peaceful here. And then she heard it. A slow and steady thudding.

Cleo put one hand over her ear. "One of the things that bothered me when I first came out here was the quiet. Now that sound is driving me crazy!"

Mattie nodded. "The drilling. J.J. would say that's the sound of money."

"Maybe it's the sound of a marriage cracking up," Cleo said softly.

"Oh, come on, you're tougher than that. At least he's not out with another woman. He's just trying to make you rich."

"No, he's trying to save the ranch."

"Maybe you're looking at things with too narrow a view." She laughed lightly. "Besides, I've heard this isn't unusual for women after their babies are born. Buck up, old girl. You've got a new hairdo and a smashing new dress. Tom will *have* to notice!"

Cleo's smile was melancholy. "I wonder when Tom will ever be home to see these wondrous new changes in me."

Fay's name belied his gender and stature. He was an enormous man with a tightly muscled body and drilling expertise to match. He was Tom's number-one man on the rig, but he was shaking his head in a way that made Tom's stomach knot up.

"I'm afraid that's about it, Tom!" Fay shouted.

"Can't we go down any deeper?" Tom's desperation was evident.

"No. I've played this one out as far as a man can. I'm sorry. I know how much this means to you." He shrugged his massive shoulders. "It's another duster."

Tom fought back tears of anger and disappointment. He was grimy from head to foot, and he could smell his own foulness. "Wait ten more minutes, and then shut her down," he shouted to Fay. And for the next ten minutes, he prayed harder than he had ever prayed in his life. The ten minutes passed and Fay called to the men to shut down well number two.

The sudden quiet was hurtful to Tom's ears. "Tell the men to take today and tomorrow off, and then check back with me."

Climbing up on a wagon loaded with pipe, he sat down and tried to decide what to do next. There was no thought of not drilling again. The only question was where? With a sigh that came up from the soles of his working boots, Tom heaved himself up and started for the ranch house.

Both Mattie and Cleo were instantly aware of the sudden silence and exchanged worried looks.

"Maybe it came in," Mattie said hopefully.

"Maybe." Cleo felt a thrill of hope. Everything would be all right again. They could do so much with the ranch and all that money.

But from the set of Tom's shoulders as he trudged to the house, she knew the news was bad, and she put on a falsely cheerful front for him. "Hello, darling," she said lightly. "Would you like a cup of coffee?"

At his nod, she poured one and put it on the table in front of his slumped figure.

It sloshed crazily as he slammed his fist down on the table. The baby began to cry from the other room, and his mother came in from her room. Robert stood in the door frame, but there was no need to explain anything to anyone.

When J.J. rode up from town, the three men held counsel out under the tree in the back yard.

"I told you up front my dad would only go for one well. I staked us to the second one, but I have no more money to offer, or believe me I would." His gaze was transparent. "But I know there's oil out there. I know it."

"Well, there's no money in this family," Tom sighed.

"And none in Cleo's either, I understand," J.J. said.

"I know where we can get the money," Robert offered quietly.

"The banks aren't going to give us a dime," Tom reminded him angrily.

"Not the bank. Leaf."

Tom spun around to stare his brother full in the face. "What are you saying?"

"Those . . . uh . . . ladies have the money, I hear. They hold money for a lot of the men 'cause they don't trust the banks. And the ladies make loans with interest and everything, just like the banks."

Tom and J.J. exchanged a look of hope.

"You know one of these women?" J.J. asked Robert.

"*Tom* does. She's been in love with him for years. I bet she'd loan him the money."

Tom's chuckle gave rise to a full-fledged, heart-lifting belly laugh, and caused the women to look out the window to see what was going on. "Robert, my boy," he said as he swiped at his eyes with the back of his hand, "there have been times when I thought you didn't know when to get in out of the rain, but when you get a good idea, you get a doozie!" He hugged his embarrassed brother in a rough playful embrace, and clapped him on the back. "It's worth a try, son."

The men fended off the women's questions with assurances that they had one more "banker" to see. "A new one in town," Tom told Cleo truthfully.

"I'll bet that doesn't make Leaf's father happy," said Cleo, who wondered why Tom's laughter seemed a bit too hearty for her little joke.

When they were in bed, Cleo asked, "Are we going to do the Houston Bank Scene?"

"No, honey, this is a new banking world. I don't think it would help the cause this time. But thank you, my love, for the offer," Tom said, and he fell asleep with dreams of riches supplied by the "businesswoman" daughter of the local banker.

# twelve

Tom groomed himself carefully, but he didn't put on his suit to wear to the "bank."

As he rode into town that afternoon, he rehearsed several possible scenarios, talking things over with his horse. "If Robert's right, and Leaf loved me once, maybe she'll give me the money for old time's sake. Or maybe she'll hate me for marrying Cleo. On the other hand, if she's a good businesswoman, she'll see an opportunity to make more money. Maybe that's what she's looking for . . . a way out of her present condition."

He did not allow himself to ponder the possibility that she might *prefer* her "fallen" life, nor what Cleo would say if she knew his plans. Besides, it was strictly business.

He gazed across the endless land and began to pour out his heart to God. "Lord, I'm way past a rock and a hard place. Maybe my motives for wanting the ranch are wrong. But I know deep in my heart that I want to make a good place for Cleo and the baby. I want to be able to hold my head up and take my place in life. Ma and Robert need taking care of, too, Lord, and this part of West Texas needs to be settled. I want to be part of all that, Lord. I realize I'm going to see a woman who isn't living a very good life right now. But she's been a friend of mine for a long time and I don't think of her as a . . . You know . . . 'businesswoman.' I'm going to her as a friend who has the money I need to save my ranch and make a good life for my family. Please help me, Lord. Please."

It wasn't hard to find Leaf's little house. But his pulse raced unnaturally as he lifted his hand to knock.

151

Wearing a fetching silk kimono trimmed in white maribou feathers, and matching mules, she looked quite lovely in the harsh afternoon sun as she opened the door. "Well, well, well. Do come in, Mr. Kinney. This is an unexpected pleasure." She led him to the fashionable couch across the room. "Drink?"

"Coffee, thanks." Tom had always felt fully in charge in Leaf's presence. With their roles reversed, he was a little off balance. He sat down on the couch and crossed his knees, putting his hat on them.

Leaf sat down beside him and handed him the coffee. "I think I'm supposed to ask you if this is business or pleasure." Her laugh was throaty and relaxed.

Tom took a sip of the hot coffee to unlock his partially paralyzed vocal cords. "It's always a pleasure to see you, Leaf."

She smiled knowingly. "I don't think so, or we would have gotten married, dear Tom, but it's nice of you to say so. Do you have a business proposition for me? Don't look so startled. Men come to me for more than my good looks, you know."

Tom blushed faintly at her candor. "I may have made a mistake about you," he said honestly. "You are lovely, and to top it off, you have a good mind."

"Water under the bridge. I'm happy for now." She refilled his cup. "You need money?"

"Yes. Enough to drill one more hole."

Leaf gave Tom a coy glance. "This is the part I like best. A man in your position will do anything to get the money. Make no mistake. I have the money to loan. But if I have any old debts I want paid off, here is the time to call them in, wouldn't you say?" She leaned closer to Tom. "I always dreamed of a time you might need me . . . back in the old days when I sat behind that desk."

Tom could smell her perfume, could feel the softness of her shoulder as she leaned against him. Her hair fell loose and brushed his face with the softness of a cloud.

"You'd be in some kind of trouble, and I'd help you, and you'd be so grateful that you'd fall in love with me and marry me," she murmured as she moved closer. "I thought you were the most wonderful man I'd ever known. My heart used to jump right out of my chest when I'd see you. And it died every time you played dead."

"Leaf, I had no idea. . . ." Beads of perspiration popped out on Tom's brow. "If only things had been different, Leaf."

"They *are* different, Tom. *I* hold all the aces." She sighed. "It feels delicious. I wouldn't trade places with any woman in the world right now." She sat back. "How far are you willing to go to get the money, Tom?" Her smile was predatory and there was a gleam in her eye.

Tom's gaze locked with hers. "I guess I'm willing to do . . . whatever it takes."

"I thought so." She positively purred with possibilities. She rose and walked over to a small desk where she pulled out a long sheet of legal paper. "There isn't any small print here, Tom. It's all very up front. The interest rate, and my cut of the royalties. Standard."

Tom reeled. "That's all?" Then he felt a little let down. She didn't want him at all. Just his money.

"Don't be disappointed, Tom. If I force you to love me, it doesn't count. I only want you if you want me. Maybe that day will come, but it isn't today." Leaf smiled at him. "I love seeing that confusion on your face. It's been a wonderful experience knowing I could shake you up a little." She laughed in delight. "You didn't know whether to run or jump into the fire with both feet."

With great chagrin, he chuckled. "You're right. I'd already considered my options on the way over here. But after I got here, it didn't seem to be too large a sacrifice, after all." His grin was still an embarrassed one. "'Course I hadn't planned on being the one to get turned down." He reached for the pen she offered and signed his name without reading the paper. "There's no need to read it. I'll go along with whatever you've got laid out for me. I'm dead out of options."

She went to the other room and returned with a wad of bills. They exchanged paper for money, and Tom started for the door.

Leaf was close on his heels and plucked at his sleeve. "There is something you can do for me, though. You were always so distant, Tom. How about one kiss to remember you by?"

It was a sweet kiss, the kind he had given Cleo on their first date, and she sighed. "Don't be too hard on yourself, Tom. You made the right choice with Cleo. She's good people."

Riding out of town, Tom fingered the wad of money. "Lord, I hadn't planned on a lesson in humility quite so severe. I found out I was willing to cheat on my wife to get the money for the ranch." His face burned with shame. "And I found out that Leaf's morals were better than mine." Tears began to stream down his face. "I don't deserve this money. I don't deserve the wonderful wife I have, nor Leaf's friendship. But most of all I'm sorry, Lord, that I failed Your test. And I promise You that I'll use this money, remembering Your mercy and goodness to me, in spite of my sinfulness. Thank You, Lord, thank You."

He was glad it was a long ride to the ranch, for it gave him time to compose himself and to come to terms with his humanness and the overwhelming grandeur of God's love.

It was close to suppertime when he rode in. He took a deep breath of the sweet air and looked at the land he owned.

The Lord had given all of it to him. He would have the money to take care of Cleo and the ranch. He could give her back all she had lost when she married him. He knew how unhappy she had been here in the wilderness. And he loved her all the more for her sacrifice.

There was oil out there. He could smell it. He had the money now to find it. He had kept his marriage vows, though it was not to his credit, and he could look Cleo in the face without deceit. "God, please show me now where to look for the oil. I know all this is in Your plan for my life, or You wouldn't have given me another chance. Show me. Lead me."

The women assumed that he had acquired the money from a legitimate bank, and the men didn't let on. And when Cleo asked Tom about it later that night, he could only tell her that the Lord had provided.

The very next day Tom's crew came back together again with the geologist. Everyone felt he had the right to put in his two cents' worth, for all of them had worked in the fields in some capacity, and had seen these men find oil.

Tom felt serene as they finally came to one accord on the exact place. He knew it would be the right one, and as the drill began to pound away at the earth, it echoed each beat of his heart. Everything would be all right now. God was on his side.


"That pounding is killing me!" Cleo muttered irritably as she poured Mattie another cup of coffee. "It'll probably wake the baby, too."

"I think she's used to it by now," Mattie consoled her. "Maybe you could use a little break. Why don't we go back to Houston and see your mother. It would do us all good to get away for a while. Your mom wanted to see little Claire so badly."

Cleo winced. "I guess Tom wouldn't even know if I was gone. There's just one thing in his life right now. Oil. I'll write Mother today."

In the privacy of their bedroom that night, Tom protested loudly. "But you can't leave now. I'm just about to strike oil!"

"That's what you've told me twice before." She faced him squarely. "Why don't you stop this foolishness? There's no oil on this ranch. There's nothing but rattlesnakes and sand! And the few cattle we have left are only here by dumb luck!

"Stop and think, Tom. Even if you do hit oil, do you expect me to raise our daughter in this solitude? No children to play with. No decent school. Nothing but loneliness. Let's go back to Houston," she begged. "You could get a good job. J.J. could surely find you something. We'd be able to give Claire all the things she's entitled to. Do you remember how lonely it was out here for you growing up? And you had Robert." Her eyes pleaded with him.

"We can have more children," he said stupidly, grabbing at anything to keep her from leaving.

She regarded him as if he had lost his mind. "Do you expect me to populate the area by myself?"

"Of course not, but now with the boom, the town will grow and there will be lots of people."

She began to pace angrily. "And I just can't wait for Claire to be best friends with all that riffraff. They have so much to offer her." Bitterness spewed out of Cleo's mouth, and words better left unsaid, were spoken. "I despise it out here in this place. Mattie is the only reason I've stayed this long. If I stay here any longer, I'll look just like your mother. Have you noticed her lately? She looks like one of those mesquites in wintertime. Is that what you want for me?

The look she turned on him was cold and unyielding.

"Tom, you're responsible for two people in this world—Claire and me. How do you plan to take care of us?"

He was stung by her sharp words, and like the mesquite thorn, they immediately began to fester in his mind. "I'm doing the best I can for both of you," he protested. "And for the rest of my family. Right now I'm breaking my back to bring in this well. Then we'll be as rich as you want to be and can do whatever you please." He wrapped his arms around her slender frame, but he could feel her resistance. "Please, honey. You know how much I love you."

She shook off his embrace and stepped away. "And you think if you tell me you love me, all our problems will melt away? Not this time. I'm thinking of Claire as much as myself. Obviously, *you* can't." She dragged out her big traveling trunk and began to pack.

Tom couldn't think of another thing to say, his anger building at her recriminations. "Women!" he spat out as he stomped from the house.

Mattie appeared at her door. "Guess I'd better get some things together. Looks like we're going home."

"And the sooner, the better," Cleo replied huffily.

"J.J. will understand if I go back with you and wait for him there," Mattie said softly. "But maybe you'd like to give yourself a day or two before we leave . . . in case something changes."

But the look on Cleo's face told her that her mind was made up. There would be no delays. She was going . . . home to Houston.

# thirteen

Cleo stood on the porch of her mother's little house and knocked. The baby was fussy and she herself felt the accumulated layers of travel dust and grime.

"My goodness, come in, come in!" Madeline took the fretful baby and soothed her while welcoming Cleo with a smile. "My girls are home," she cooed to her namesake, and tactfully didn't ask about Tom.

With the baby asleep and Cleo bathed and changed, the two women sat down in the small living room with a glass of iced tea.

"This was a special treat at the ranch," Cleo said, taking a sip. "It was saved for dances or parties." She rolled the damp glass across her forehead and sighed. "It's been like living with a foot in two different worlds."

"And to what do I owe this visit to our world?" her mother asked. "I wanted to see the baby, but I didn't think you'd be able to bring her this soon."

Cleo fought the tears that formed in her eyes. "I'm not as good a wife as you were. I couldn't take it anymore."

"Don't nominate me for sainthood, my dear. I took my own little 'vacations' away from your father now and again. I think that may have been one of the reasons we stayed married for so long." Madeline smiled. "Sometimes couples can have too much time together. Everyone needs to have a little breathing space occasionally."

Cleo abruptly changed the subject. "Mother, you look wonderful. And content. I've missed you. Now tell me everything that's going on."

Madeline beamed. "Well, I feel very well, I'm learning to live by myself, and as you can see there is very little maintenance to this small home. I cook simple meals, shop a little, play too much bridge, and see a few old friends." She patted Cleo's hand. "It is a fact of life that when one is widowed, one doesn't receive the invitations one used to receive. I'm an odd number at a dinner party. And, you know, I do think some of those women act as though I'm after their husband now that I'm not married." She laughed. "As if one of those old goats could ever replace your father!"

Cleo laughed delightedly. "You could give them a run for their money, Mother. You're still very beautiful. You'd be quite a catch."

"Oh, everything changes, dear," Madeline said, sobering. "People and situations don't remain the same. I want to warn you that you should be prepared to find things different, too. At this late date, I'm just finding out who my real friends are."

Cleo shrugged. "Well, dear old Mattie never changes. We had the most wonderful time together . . . almost like the old days. With the men away so much, we sort of re-lived the past. Oh, Mother, let me tell you about the oil boom in Kermit!" And she regaled her mother with anecdotes.

As the laughter subsided, Cleo hesitantly told about her fight with Tom.

"Oh, my darling, I wish I had a magic wand to wave and make everything perfect for you. This little vacation will give you time to think things out. I'm sorry it took this for us to be together, but I'm thrilled to see the little one. She's beautiful. She reminds me so much of you as a baby." Love shone brightly from her face.

Taking her cue, Cleo filled her mother in on Claire's birth

and Tante Olga's loving care. And there were stories of other kindnesses from the West Texas folks. But Cleo's happy face sobered as she approached the next part of her story.

"I don't think I can say this without sounding like a snob, but I think you'll understand, Mother. The people out there are kind. But it's not the place I want Claire to grow up in. I want her to have polish like you, knowledge of good books and music. Manners that will take her anywhere. Clothes and friends. A good college."

"You want her to be like you, my sweet. You are all those things." Madeline smiled gently.

"If I am, it's because you gave them to me. I want no less for my own daughter." She fingered the wedding ring on her hand. "Tom doesn't understand."

"So you feel you must choose between your husband and your daughter?"

"I hadn't thought of it that way, but . . . I'm afraid so."

A frown of distress furrowed Madeline's brow. "There's an old saying about not throwing away the baby with the bath water. Perhaps if you think in terms of compromise, you won't have to choose one or the other. Let me remind you of one thing: You promised on your wedding day in front of God to cling to Tom in sickness and in health . . . in good times *and* in bad. . . ." She put her arm around Cleo. "Darling, I've seen Tom look at you. I've seen the things he endured here to make you happy. He's a good man, Cleo. I don't think you'd ever find anyone who loves you more. Maybe he's not on track right now. Maybe he's put you second place in his life. But that's no reason to throw away what you have together."

She sat back against the soft cushions. "I've found that life is like a roller coaster. Sometimes you're up and sometimes you're down. But the roller coaster keeps moving.

Life keeps moving. You weather the bad times and savor the good. And as you learn to live together, there is steadily more good than bad. Until near the end of your time together, it's so good that it's almost unbearable when one leaves the other. . . ." Tears spilled down her cheeks.

"Oh, Mother, I'm so sorry!" Cleo threw her arms around her mother and hugged her hard.

Madeline dabbed her eyes with her hanky. "No, don't feel sorry for me. I've had a wonderful life. And I plan to go on having a full life.

"Cleo, perhaps the one thing I regret is not speaking more often to your father about God. He was such a reserved man. So private. I felt as though he had put God in some sort of compartment. It was something we just didn't speak of. Now I wish I knew how he felt about dying. Was he frightened? Did he think he was going to heaven? Cleo, don't make that mistake with Tom. Share your faith with him. Talk to him. Invite God into your home. We gave you everything . . . except the most important thing . . . a mother and father who prayed openly and sought God's direction."

Madeline's eyes glowed with conviction. "How odd that this late in my life, my faith is beginning to flower. Imagine . . . an old lady like me in the flush of an awakening. I am preparing now for my own death, and it's not frightening at all. I'm at peace now. I want that for you long before you get to be my age." She looked into her daughter's eyes. "You live in an uncertain land. You need God to help you through the years ahead."

Cleo nodded, but in her room later, she couldn't help wondering if the strain of her father's death had caused a true spiritual awakening, or if her mother was grasping at religion to shore up her faltering spirits. Still, the things she had shared with Cleo were true. Things she needed to think about seriously. God had become much more important to

Cleo since her move to West Texas. She found herself praying without formality over the smallest things.

But she blushed to think she hadn't prayed at all about this enormous rift with Tom. *I'm sorry, Lord. I was so mad I didn't think, I just acted. But I need time to think all this out, Lord. Both Tom and I are going to have to make some changes in our lives. Help me to be wise. I do love him, but he makes me so mad! Lead me, Lord. And keep Tom safe until we can work all this out.*

The next day Cleo called Mattie and they set up a luncheon at one of their favorite restaurants with some of their old friends. Cleo felt like a girl again as she dressed carefully.

"Hey, I like that dress," Mattie said smilingly when she slipped into the passenger seat of Cleo's little Ford. "Did you get that here?"

"Of course not, dahling," Cleo said in the exaggerated dialect of the very rich, "I bought it in the most expensive store in all of West Texas. You wouldn't know it. It's much too exclusive for the Houston set."

Mattie giggled. "I don't think you've changed at all, dahling."

They walked into the restaurant. "It feels wonderful to be dining in a lovely place again. I've missed all this," Cleo told Mattie.

Mattie wrinkled her nose. "That's funny. I never noticed you can almost smell money in the air here. And talk about class!" She glanced around. "I don't remember feeling this way about this place before."

Cleo didn't wait to hear Mattie's remarks. Her mind was on the good time ahead. "Don't be silly. Oh, there are the girls over there."

The conversation swirled about the table as the friends caught up on the latest news. Talk of horses and men and trips to Europe and clothes and parties. Muted references as to who was misbehaving with whom, accompanied by giggles. It was all too stimulating for Cleo.

During a lull, she told her ranch tales, shading them to sound like a great adventure, or even a safari to a foreign land. Once she caught sight of Mattie's puckered brow, but she staunchly refused to tell her friends the real story.

As they left to go home, Mattie shot her a look of disgust. "Now *that* was an uplifting experience."

Cleo bridled. "Well, I had a wonderful time. It was great to hear about all the things that are going on."

Mattie shook her head. "I never noticed before, but what I heard today was a lot of tripe."

"Mattie! It was just girl talk."

"We're not girls anymore, Cleo. If you took all the gossip we heard in the beauty shop in Kermit, tied it up in fancy wrappings, and dropped it in the middle of that high-class café, you'd have exactly the same thing."

Cleo was shocked. "How can you say that! They were talking about Europe and concerts and glamorous parties!"

"They were talking about *people*, not cathedrals or paintings or music. Except for her correct grammar, Betty St. James sounded just like those two beauticians."

"Mattie, you've become the ultimate snob!" Cleo accused.

Mattie caught Cleo's arm and jerked her around to face her. "I met some nice people out there. They were honest and real and they had goals in their lives. They were building something worth dying for. Those 'girls' in there are just that—girls. And it makes me sick to think I sounded like that myself not too long ago. Thank you for inviting me to the land of the real. And if you had one ounce of sense, you'd catch the next train back to the ranch, get down on your knees and beg Tom to forgive you and take you back!"

Cleo felt as if she had been slapped hard in the face. "Mattie, what's gotten into you?"

"I think maybe one of us has finally grown up." Her eyes reflected a deep understanding. "And I think it's me."

There was little else to say on the way home, but when Cleo let Mattie out in front of her house, she said, "You think hard on what I said about Tom. There isn't a better man around. You're a dope if you let him slip out of your life because of some silly set of values you learned as a kid."

To say that Cleo's sleep was fitful that night would be an understatement. Her head felt like a giant mixing bowl, with thoughts and voices tossing and tumbling inside. But when she awoke in the morning, her decision had jelled. She loved Tom. And no matter what, she wanted to live with him. Instead of being fatigued, she felt renewed and energetic, eager to get back to the hub of her world.

Cleo kissed her mother and Mattie good-bye at the train depot. This time the tears were happy ones.

"I'm going to miss little Claire," Madeline said. "And you, too, my darling. But I know you're happy, and that's all that matters."

"Mother, it's easy to get on a train and come to see us. I promise you an exciting and unique experience." Cleo smiled. "And my Mattie. What would I have done without you?" She hugged her red-haired friend tightly as her mother held the baby one last time.

Mattie only shrugged. "Oh, you'd have figured it out eventually. I just gave you a shortcut," she said with false modesty. Then she whispered in Cleo's ear, "Don't forget what I told you. You have the best guy I ever met. Don't let anyone or anything come between you. And invite me back to the ranch soon. I'm hankering to dance with old Crook!" Mattie was crying openly as Cleo mounted the steps to the train.

And after the baby was asleep, Cleo leaned against the window of the train, feeling the hypnotic rocking of the train as it swayed its way over the tracks back to Tom.

Cleo had put on a brave front with those two. But now she wondered what was waiting for her at home. What if Tom didn't want her back? What if she had gone too far? She moaned silently as she recalled all the hurtful things she had slung at him the night she had left.

*Father,* she prayed silently, please help me. *I want Tom's love back . . . and our home and family. I have no idea what to do next, but when I look back at my life, somehow I feel You've been there all along, guiding me and making things happen. How else could Tom and I have met? I'm at the bottom of the cup, Lord. I won't make deals with You, but I will promise that if I get the chance, I will be what You want me to be. But I can't do it without Your help.* There wasn't any outward sign that God had heard her prayers, but she added another petition. *And help me to love Tom's mother, even if she seems impossible.*

Cleo fell asleep against the window, feeling a measure of relief that she was no longer alone. God would help her set everything straight.

Despite her prayer on the train and the restful nap, Cleo's stomach was in knots when she reached the sandy dunes outside Monahans. She was in a foreign land again. And her harp was still on the willow. It would be, until she knew Tom still loved her and wanted her.

The town looked busier than it had the last time she saw it. Spillover from the Kermit boom, I guess. "Well, Baby Claire," she said, nuzzling the child's downy head, "all we have to do is find someone to take us to the ranch."

Glancing across the street, she noticed the Holman House,

a restaurant that seemed to be enjoying a thriving business. She was starving to death. Leaving her luggage, she walked over for a good meal and a chance to inquire whether some-one might be someone going her way. She could always hire someone, if worse came to worst.

Inside, she heard a familiar voice coming from the dining room. Fattie Smallwood, napkin tucked neatly under his chin and covering his ample chest, stood immediately as she entered.

"Why, Mrs. Kinney, er, Cleo! What a wonderful surprise!" He offered her an empty chair beside him and took the baby from her arms, cooing softly to the child.

"Always room for one more," Mrs. Holman called out from the kitchen.

"Fattie, is there any chance you might be going out to-ward the ranch?" Cleo asked.

"Why, ma'am, even if I wasn't, I'd make a special trip just for you," Fattie said gallantly.

He was much too kind, Cleo knew, to ask any more per-sonal questions, such as, What was she doing getting off a train by herself with no one to meet her?

Fattie loaded Cleo's things in the wagon and clucked the mules to an easy gait, swaying over the sand like a boat gliding, if somewhat roughly, over an earth-toned sea.

"Beautiful country, ain't it?" he observed with a smile of satisfaction.

With great surprise, Cleo realized that it was. "I don't think I ever considered it so before. But I suppose it is beautiful, in its own way."

"You know ma'am, beauty is a funny thing. I've met up with some women so homely they'd have to rub their faces with barbecue sauce to get the dogs to lick 'em. And I've seen women near as beautiful as you." Cleo smiled at his compliment. "But you know as well as I do that unless there's a reason to love the inside of that woman, neither one of 'em is appealing."

He looked around. "Now take this country out here. It's sort of the homely one, some say. I like to think of her beauty bein' in her spareness. There ain't nothing extra on her. She's lean and clean. There ain't a lot of stuff to take my mind off o' lovin' her for jest what she is. Restful. Oh, I know it takes a heap o' work to make a livin' out here, but after it's done, she's restful to be with."

Cleo's eyes scanned the endless horizon and thought of the busyness of Houston's streets. There was so much to love about Houston, so many happy memories, and some sad ones. And she loved that city. But with clearing eyes she saw what Fattie was talking about. And she thought about what Mattie had said. "They are building something out there. Something worth dying for." Cleo felt her pulse quicken with a new beat. "Thank you, Fattie."

"Ahh, I was just ramblin', ma'am. I oughta pay ya to listen."

They rolled on, past the China Springs windmill, and Cleo remembered the first time she had seen it with Tom. "How come this one is named China Springs?"

"Some say it's because one woman went crazy when they camped beside it and broke every dish she had in the wagon against its base." He joined her in a chuckle.

"I can understand how she felt," Cleo admitted.

"Funny thing about windmills," Fattie observed. "They all have their own sounds, you know. Jest like people's voices. Some of 'em sound lonesome and some of 'em have a comforting sound, like a mama croonin' to her baby."

Cleo shivered in the warm air.

"No need to feel spooked, ma'am. Them windmills all look like a tree of life to me."

It was nearly dusk, that time in the West when the sand

creates an odd alchemy of nature that can be duplicated nowhere else on earth. Cleo saw it now. The rays of the setting sun, sifting through the sand and molded into unbelievably gorgeous hues of red, orange, yellow, pinks and purples, splashed against a canvas of fluffy white clouds just above the horizon. It was truly breathtaking.

"What a wonderful homecoming," she breathed, as much to God as to Fattie on the wagon seat beside her.

As they neared the ranch, sounds of music could be heard and lights twinkled on in the coming darkness.

"Looks like they're havin' a git-together at your place," Fattie said.

As they drew closer, Cleo could see that a full-fledged party was in progress. "Must be our turn to host the dance."

She could pick out Tom's broad-shouldered frame in the distance as he mingled with the guests under the string of lanterns. He was heartbreakingly handsome. As if feeling her eyes on him, he turned and saw her coming.

He loped to meet her, his face flushed, a big grin spread from ear to ear. "Cleo! Cleo! You're back!" He swung her down from the wagon as Fattie climbed down and took the baby out of the little nest he had made for her in the back.

"My darling, Cleo," Tom whispered against her hair.

"I'm sorry, Tom . . ."

"Not now, Cleo. Not ever. Honey, we're rich! We've struck oil!"

"Tom, put me down! Hold me close." Her mind as well as her body was spinning. "You really did strike oil?"

He nodded. "And we're having a party to celebrate." He led her into the yard, where Cleo was welcomed as if she had only been on a short trip to town to buy supplies.

Her mouth fell open in surprise when she saw Mrs. Kinney, dancing and laughing and looking fifteen years younger.

"Sometimes it only takes the rain to make the cactus

bloom," said Tom happily.

Catching Cleo's eye, Mrs. Kinney abandoned her partner and came to greet her. "Welcome, home, Cleo! And where's my granddaughter? I need to see how much she's grown!"

All the noise and confusion awakened Claire, but she went into Mrs. Kinney's arms without a whimper, eyes round with wonder. "Now you dance with your husband, child. I'm a good hand with babies, if I do say so. Besides, I need to catch up on things with Hiram . . . uh . . . Fattie." And she gave Tom a meaningful look.

Everyone was there. Crook asked Cleo for a waltz, and if she had been on a ballroom floor in Paris, she couldn't have had a better partner. "Cowboys are the best dancers in the world," she told him.

"Yes, ma'am," Crook agreed, "it's from stayin' on horses and tiptoein' over trouble."

And then she was back in Tom's arms, while the fiddle music swirled the women's skirts and lifted the men's boots. His arms felt so good around her. His smell was familiar, as was the contour of his body. She snuggled against him, cherishing the knowledge of him. "Tom, the Lord has brought all this about, I know it. I've learned I can't live my life without His guidance and care."

"You're not the only one who's learned a few things," he confessed. "If you only knew how many times I've prayed lately, most of all, that He would send you back to me. He's given us everything, Cleo."

She smiled up into his eyes. "Everything. So much that, even if we hadn't struck oil, we'd be rich!" She thought of the psalm Tante Olga had quoted to her when Claire was born, and she laughed. "I want to go out to the Sand Hills, out by the big water seep."

Tom pulled away to look down into her radiant face. "Whatever for, my dearest?"

"I want to take down my harp from the willow tree. I can sing the Lord's song in a foreign land. No more regrets. No more doubts. I'm home."

# *A Letter To Our Readers*

Dear Reader:

In order that we might better contribute to your reading enjoyment, we would appreciate your taking a few minutes to respond to the following questions. When completed, please return to the following:

Rebecca Germany, Editor
Heartsong Presents
P.O. Box 719
Uhrichsville, Ohio 44683

1. Did you enjoy reading *Song of Captivity*?
   ☐ Very much. I would like to see more books by this author!
   ☐ Moderately
   I would have enjoyed it more if _____

   _____

2. Are you a member of *Heartsong Presents*? Yes No
   If no, where did you purchase this book? _____

   _____

3. What influenced your decision to purchase this book? (Circle those that apply.)

   | | |
   |---|---|
   | Cover | Back cover copy |
   | Title | Friends |
   | Publicity | Other _____ |

4. On a scale from 1 (poor) to 10 (superior), please rate the following elements.

___Heroine     ___Plot

___Hero     ___Inspirational theme

___Setting     ___Secondary characters

5. What settings would you like to see covered in *Heartsong Presents* books?

_____

_____

6. What are some inspirational themes you would like to see treated in future books?_____

_____

_____

7. Would you be interested in reading other *Heartsong Presents* titles?     Yes     No

8. Please circle your age range:
   Under 18     18-24     25-34
   35-45     46-55     Over 55

9. How many hours per week do you read? _____

Name _____

Occupation _____

Address _____

City _____ State _____ Zip _____

# ····· Hearts♥ng ·········

**ROMANCE IS CHEAPER BY THE DOZEN!**

Any 12 *Heartsong Presents* titles for only $26.95 *

Buy any assortment of twelve *Heartsong Presents* titles and save 25% off of the already discounted price of $2.95 each!

*plus $1.00 shipping and handling per order and sales tax where applicable.

## *HEARTSONG PRESENTS TITLES AVAILABLE NOW:*

___HP 1 A TORCH FOR TRINITY, *Colleen L. Reece*
___HP 2 WILDFLOWER HARVEST, *Colleen L. Reece*
___HP 3 RESTORE THE JOY, *Sara Mitchell*
___HP 4 REFLECTIONS OF THE HEART, *Sally Laity*
___HP 5 THIS TREMBLING CUP, *Marlene Chase*
___HP 6 THE OTHER SIDE OF SILENCE, *Marlene Chase*
___HP 7 CANDLESHINE, *Colleen L. Reece*
___HP 8 DESERT ROSE, *Colleen L. Reece*
___HP 9 HEARTSTRINGS, *Irene B. Brand*
___HP10 SONG OF LAUGHTER, *Lauraine Snelling*
___HP11 RIVER OF FIRE, *Jacquelyn Cook*
___HP13 PASSAGE OF THE HEART, *Kjersti Hoff Baez*
___HP14 A MATTER OF CHOICE, *Susannah Hayden*
___HP15 WHISPERS ON THE WIND, *Maryn Langer*
___HP16 SILENCE IN THE SAGE, *Colleen L. Reece*
___HP17 LLAMA LADY, *VeraLee Wiggins*
___HP18 ESCORT HOMEWARD, *Eileen M. Berger*
___HP19 A PLACE TO BELONG, *Janelle Jamison*
___HP20 SHORES OF PROMISE, *Kate Blackwell*
___HP21 GENTLE PERSUASION, *Veda Boyd Jones*
___HP22 INDY GIRL, *Brenda Bancroft*
___HP23 GONE WEST, *Kathleen Karr*
___HP24 WHISPERS IN THE WILDERNESS, *Colleen L. Reece*
___HP25 REBAR, *Mary Carpenter Reid*
___HP26 MOUNTAIN HOUSE, *Mary Louise Colln*
___HP27 BEYOND THE SEARCHING RIVER, *Jacquelyn Cook*
___HP28 DAKOTA DAWN, *Lauraine Snelling*
___HP29 FROM THE HEART, *Sara Mitchell*
___HP30 A LOVE MEANT TO BE, *Brenda Bancroft*
___HP31 DREAM SPINNER, *Sally Laity*
___HP32 THE PROMISED LAND, *Kathleen Karr*
___HP33 SWEET SHELTER, *VeraLee Wiggins*
___HP34 UNDER A TEXAS SKY, *Veda Boyd Jones*
___HP35 WHEN COMES THE DAWN, *Brenda Bancroft*
___HP36 THE SURE PROMISE, *JoAnn A. Grote*
___HP37 DRUMS OF SHELOMOH, *Yvonne Lehman*
___HP38 A PLACE TO CALL HOME, *Eileen M. Berger*
___HP39 RAINBOW HARVEST, *Norene Morris*
___HP40 PERFECT LOVE, *Janelle Jamison*
___HP41 FIELDS OF SWEET CONTENT, *Norma Jean Lutz*
___HP42 SEARCH FOR TOMORROW, *Mary Hawkins*
(If ordering from this page, please remember to include it with the order form.)